HARRY MOON

HALLOWEEN NIGHTMARES

by
Mark Andrew Poe

Illustrations by Christina Weidman

rabbit publishers

Halloween Nightmares (Harry Moon)
by Mark Andrew Poe
© Copyright 2017 by Mark Andrew Poe. All rights reserved.

No part of this book may be reproduced in any written, electronic recording, or photocopying without written permission of the publisher, except for brief quotations in articles, reviews or pages where permission is specifically granted by the publisher.

Rabbit Publishers
1624 W. Northwest Highway
Arlington Heights, IL 60004

Illustrations by Christina Weidman
Cover design by Megan Black
Interior Design by Lewis Design & Marketing
Creative Consultants: David Kirkpatrick, Thom Black, and Paul Lewis

ISBN: 978-1-943785-63-6

10 9 8 7 6 5 4 3 2 1

1. Fiction - Action and Adventure 2. Children's Fiction
First Edition
Printed in U.S.A.

Don't worry.
I've got you covered.

~ Rabbit

Table of Contents

PREFACE

Halloween visited the little town of Sleepy Hollow and never left.

Many moons ago, a sly and evil mayor found the powers of darkness helpful in building Sleepy Hollow into "Spooky Town," one of the country's most celebrated attractions. Now, years later, a young eighth-grade wizard, Harry Moon, is chosen by the powers of light to do battle against the mayor and his evil consorts.

Welcome to the world of Harry Moon and his amazing adventures. Darkness may have found a home in Sleepy Hollow, but if young Harry Moon has anything to say about it, darkness won't be staying.

FAMILY, FRIENDS & FOES

Harry Moon

Harry is the thirteen-year-old hero of Sleepy Hollow. He is a gifted magician who is learning to use his abilities and understand what it means to possess the real magic.

An unlikely hero, Harry is shorter than his classmates and has a shock of inky, black hair. He loves his family and his town. Along with his friend Rabbit, Harry is determined to bring Sleepy Hollow back to its true and wholesome glory.

Rabbit

Now you see him. Now you don't. Rabbit is Harry Moon's friend. Some see him. Most can't.

Rabbit is a large, black-and-white, lop-eared Harlequin rabbit. As Harry has discovered, having a friend like Rabbit has its consequences. Never stingy with advice and counsel, Rabbit always has Harry's back as Harry battles the evil that has overtaken Sleepy Hollow.

II

Honey Moon

She's a ten-year-old, sassy spitfire. And she's Harry's little sister. Honey likes to say she goes where she is needed, and sometimes this takes her into the path of danger.

Honey never gives in and never gives up when it comes to righting a wrong. Honey always looks out for her friends. Honey does not like that her town has been plunged into a state of eternal Halloween and is even afraid of the evil she feels lurking all around. But if Honey has anything to say about it, evil will not be sticking around.

III

Samson Dupree

Samson is the enigmatic owner of the Sleepy Hollow Magic Shoppe. He is Harry's mentor and friend. When needed, Samson teaches Harry new tricks and helps him understand his gift of magic.

Samson arranged for Rabbit to become Harry's sidekick and friend. Samson is a timeless, eccentric man who wears purple robes, red slippers, and a gold crown. Sometimes, Samson shows up in mysterious ways. He even appeared to Harry's mother shortly after Harry's birth.

Mary Moon

Strong, fair, and spiritual, Mary Moon is Harry and Honey's mother. She is also mother to two-year-old Harvest. Mary is married to John Moon.

Mary is learning to understand Harry and his destiny. So far, she is doing a good job letting Harry and Honey fight life's battles. She's grateful that Rabbit has come alongside to support and counsel her. But like all moms, Mary often finds it difficult to let her children walk their own paths. Mary is a nurse at Sleepy Hollow Hospital.

John Moon

John is the dad. He's a bit of a nerd. He works as an IT professional, and sometimes he thinks he would love it if his children followed in his footsteps. But he respects that Harry, Honey, and possibly Harvest will need to go their own way. John owns a classic sports car he calls Emma.

Titus Kligore

Titus is the mayor's son. He is a bully of the first degree but also quite conflicted when it comes to Harry. The two have managed to forge a tentative friendship, although Titus will assert his bully strength on Harry from time to time.

Titus is big. He towers over Harry. But in a kind of David vs. Goliath way, Harry has learned which tools are best to counteract Titus's assaults while most of the Sleepy Hollow kids fear him. Titus would probably rather not be a bully, but with a dad like Maximus Kligore, he feels trapped in the role.

Maximus Kligore

The epitome of evil, nastiness, and greed, Maximus Kligore is the mayor of Sleepy Hollow. To bring in the cash, Maximus turned the town into the nightmarish Halloween attraction it is today.

He commissions the evil-tinged celebrations in town. Maximus is planning to take Sleepy Hollow with him to Hell. But will he? He knows Harry Moon is a threat to his dastardly ways, but try as he might, he has yet to rid himself of Harry's meddling.

Kligore lives on Folly Farm and owns most of the town, including the town newspaper.

INKLING

There was trouble afoot in Sleepy Hollow. Harry could feel it, although he couldn't quite put his finger on what was causing his uneasiness.

There, on top of his bed, a brown box sat. A note from his mom was taped to it. "I thought we'd change it up this year," the note read.

Harry knew what was coming. He did not even have to open the cardboard box with the cellophane top. But he did, anyway. It was his Elvis Gold costume from last year.

But this year, the front of the costume was covered in silver chains, which Harry figured was an homage to one of Gold's most famous tricks—the escape from the lake while locked in chains.

Harry Moon moaned with the anguish that only a kid in middle school could truly understand. "I'm in eighth grade," he said to his reflection in the pine-framed mirror above his study desk. "I'll change it up all right!" He looked at his chin carefully for any possible sign of new whisker growth. He withered with the realization that absolutely nothing had changed since he had last looked in the boys' restroom after fifth-period science.

He flopped on his bed. *Change it up. I am really gonna change it up.* But, he would have to tell his folks his plans. And what Harry Moon planned was way too important to blurt out at dinner. Besides, he just knew his know-it-all sister, Honey, could not be part of this. He had to go stealth. He needed to assemble his mom and dad and have a private "big guy" talk, as his dad was fond of calling them.

After dinner with the usual suspects (his family), Harry waited in his bedroom until seven thirty when he was scheduled to meet his parents in his dad's study. Harry had an English lit test the next day, but there was no way he could study until his meeting was over. These kinds of meetings always made Harry nervous, and this one was no exception. In fact, he felt so nervous he thought he might vomit into the cardboard costume box. He looked into the box. *There is not enough room for all my barf.*

For a while, he stared into the cardboard box where the "change ups" from previous years were stored. There was the gold-sequined jumpsuit—the trademark outfit of Elvis Gold, the most famous illusionist in the world. There was the black pompadour wig with long sideburns. As he stared, he saw the other "change ups" his mom had provided—blue lapels on the jumpsuit, a shiny red belt, and gold-painted tennies.

Looking at all the work his mom had done for him over all those Halloweens only made him feel worse about what he was going to tell them.

He checked his watch for the umpteenth time.

Finally, it was time.

It was quiet in the house when Harry walked down the stairway to face the music with his parents. Honey Moon was in her room, no doubt doing her homework. She was a good student but bragged to Harry about it every single day. Not cool. His brother, Harvest Moon, was asleep. He needed more sack time than Harry and Honey because he was only two. Their normally noisy dog, Half Moon, was in the backyard, quietly walking off his dinner in his typical, dozy, I-ate-too-much stupor. So cool. Conditions were just right for the most important "big guy" talk of Harry's life.

Harry only asked for a family meeting when it was really important, so he thought his parents would be just as nervous as him. He anticipated his dad would pace the floor. He imagined his mom would wring her hands like someone in one of those old black-and-white movies.

Instead, he found a very different set of parents sitting at the little mahogany game table playing Clue while they waited for him.

"Ah ha!" cried Mary Moon, as she giddily read her card.

"Secret passage!" She slammed her pawn down on the Ball Room space.

"Oh you are a crafty one, Mrs. Peacock!"

said Harry's dad, John Moon. He was lanky and tall like a Slim Jim, the absolute opposite of Harry, who was short for his age.

"Crafty and clever, Professor Plum," Mary said as she fussed with her pretty blonde hair and struck a haughty pose and laughed.

They were so enthralled with their game of Clue that Harry had to clear his throat to grab their attention.

"Aer-ammm," he said. It didn't come out the way he had hoped. It sounded like he was gargling marbles.

"Harry," his mom said as she straightened up.

"My Moon Man!" John Moon said. Harry noticed the name immediately. This is what his dad called him when his dad was a tad nervous. Harry felt a little better now that he knew that he was not the only one stressed.

John Moon rose from his chair. He walked

behind Harry and closed the wooden door to the rest of the house. The room was aptly named the Reading Room. The built-in shelves were crammed with books. Ancient books. New books. Books with dust covers. Everyone in the Moon family was a reader.

This was it. Big guy time!

"What's wrong, sweetheart?" Mary Moon said as she sat down on the sofa. Her voice was gentle and soothing.

"I hate to break up a good thing," Harry said gently, "but I have to."

"What's to break up?" John Moon said. He shrugged and adjusted his spiffy tech glasses as he stared at his son.

"I mean, I know how you like to be Cinderella," Harry said to his mother. "And I know you like Dracula, Dad," he said looking at his father. "And . . . and I always liked being Elvis Gold."

"He's your idol," Mary Moon said. "Did you get my note? Did you see the chains?"

Harry nodded. "Well, the Moon family has always been a team," he said, "and I have great memories of us at this time of year." He glanced out the window toward the back yard. "Dad, it was like yesterday you hid in the old oak and jumped down on me in your bat wings." Harry chuckled. "I needed twelve stitches. And Mom, I will never forget the time you showed me how to execute a perfect fox trot for the sixth-grade Halloween dance. You were so patient even when I was slamming your toes."

Harry watched a smile stretch across his mom's face. He looked at his feet and took a deep breath. "But, that's it for me." He looked up. "I have to do it my way this year." Harry got choked up again. He tried to clear his throat. But there was that awful gurgle sound again.

9

"What are you saying, sweetheart?" Mary asked.

"This year, I will be going as myself," Harry said with all the strength and confidence he could muster.

"Yourself? I hope you are always yourself," said John.

Mary Moon put her hand on John's shoulder. "He means he's not going trick-or-treating any more in costume."

"I'm not going trick-or-treating *at all*."

Harry saw his mom's eyes flash as mothers' eyes do. She was already working on the solution.

"Will you at least take Honey trick-or-treating in your regular clothes?" Mary Moon asked with a certain amount of negotiating wisdom. "You know how she likes going with you."

"If you really believe that, Mom, I'll take Honey trick-or-treating. But as myself."

"So you've gone beyond Elvis Gold? I understand, I suppose," John Moon said. "After all, you did flatten him with your magic on our living room floor."

"It's not that, Dad."

"And you are only becoming stronger with your magic," Mary Moon said, watching Harry carefully as he stood completely still.

"I hope so, Mom."

"Then why don't you want to have Halloween fun with us?"

Harry shook his head. "It's hard to put a finger on it. There is something I have to do. There is trouble around us. I cannot quite put my finger on it. I am afraid it may involve Mayor Maximus Kligore. As you know, I have had some pretty gnarly concerns."

"Those are only concerns, Harry," said Harry's dad. "They have not been proven."

"I have to rise to it, Dad," said Harry. "I have to snuff it out. Rightly or wrongly, I have taken the call."

"The call from who?" asked John Moon. "You're only twelve!"

"I am thirteen, Dad."

"Oh, yes, sorry."

"He is speaking metaphorically," Mary Moon explained.

"I am speaking of Rabbit," Harry said, fidgeting with one of the game pieces.

"What does Rabbit have to do with this?" John Moon asked.

"Rabbit has a plan. It doesn't involve a costume to be worn by me or any of my friends on the Good Mischief Team," answered Harry.

"What will you do?"

"Stick with Rabbit."

Mary Moon sighed. She rubbed her hand across the bubbly, embroidered fabric on the sofa. "Just to clarify, Harry. I know this is small potatoes in the cosmological battle of the spirit world, but . . . remember you have agreed to at least walk with your sister."

"If that's what she wants, Mom."

"Oh, Honey wants her older brother all right. She'll be glad to hear that."

Harry breathed a sigh of relief. He did not puke after all. The big guy talk was over. And he had business to deal with this Halloween night.

13

14

DOES THE WIND
SLAM THE DOOR?

I t was Sunday morning. Harry was singing with his family at Old North Church. In the crook of his arm, Harry held his little brother,

Harvest. While Harry sang, he emphasized the words of the hymn to his pudgy, round-faced brother. Harry made Os with his mouth and Es with his grin.

Little Harvest was too preoccupied with Harry's head to learn a new song that Sunday. He patted Harry's hair with both hands as if it were a parade drum. Despite the happy surroundings, Harry, gifted with the ability to see what most of us cannot, turned his head toward the double oak doors at the back of the historic church.

Darkness was approaching. He couldn't see it, but he could feel it. Harry shivered from the chill.

The stone walls of the almost four-hundred-year-old church flickered with bright candlelight. There were white candles on the altar and vigil lights beneath the cross.

Mary Moon, unlike her son, did not have Harry's special sight, although like most moms with sons in middle school, she gave the impression that she had eyes in the back of her head. Her children—Harry, Harvest, and Honey—marveled at her ability. Even their dog, Half Moon, sensed her all-knowing eyes. Mary reached over and gently took Harvest's hands and pulled them down from Harry's head. She wanted Harvest to pay attention to the words of the hymn.

"Harvest Moon, I want you to listen to the words," Mary said in a soft whisper as her husband, John Moon, smiled and continued to sing.

> This is my Father's world,
> and to my list'ning ears
> All nature sings, and round me rings
> the music of the spheres.

The hymn was written by a nineteenth-century pastor and naturalist, Maltbie D. Babcock. Pastor Babcock had been famous in Upstate New York because he often took hikes in the mountains. Surrounded by the high peaks and clouds, the pastor would ponder the wonders of life reflected in the beauty of nature.

> This is my Father's world,
> The birds their carols raise,
> The morning light, the lily white,
> Declare their Maker's praise.

Harvest, a budding naturalist himself perhaps, loved playing in the grass and discovering ladybugs and caterpillars. If he did understand the words of the hymn, Harry was certain he would have appreciated them.

Outside the quaint church, a golden Flying Lady rolled through the corner of Maple Street and Mt. Sinai Road. That would be the classic hood ornament perched on a beautiful black luxury car—the Phantom Lustro. This Flying Lady or, as she was also known, The Spirit of Desire, was a golden statuette made of twenty-four karat gold, anchored firmly on the hood. The hood ornament was a symbol of power. Very few people in the world could afford such an expensive automobile.

The black Phantom Lustro pulled up in

18

front of the Old North Church as the singing continued, the people unaware.

This is my Father's world,
the battle is not done . . .

"That's right," said the voice inside the black Phantom. "That battle is far from over! Am I right, ladies?"

"Right, Boss Man," Cherry Tomato answered. She chortled like a loon.

19

Inside the car, the rough-looking, beady-eyed mayor of Sleepy Hollow, Maximus Kligore, stared intently out the window. Mayor Kligore happened to be one of the few in Sleepy Hollow who could afford a car like the Lustro, although, honestly, no one could figure out where he got all his money. Mayor Kligore was sitting in the passenger seat next to his assistant and driver, the pert Cherry Tomato.

At first glance inside the car, you'd think the town's business leaders were having a meeting, but they were not. It was a meeting of the We Drive By Night Company. In the backseat were the attractive managers of the novelty store, Fire Magic, located at 999 Gehenna Street in Boston. They were the fetching Booboo Hoodoo ("I'm Booboo Hoodoo with the voodoo," she would always say when she greeted customers) and pink-suited Ruby Rutabaker.

The Mayor and his happy passengers were celebrating Cherry Tomato's birthday. Ruby pulled a small but fancy-looking cake from a bakery box foiled in gold leaf. It had six unlit candles.

"Does anyone have a match?" Ruby asked.

No one did.

"I'll handle that," Mayor Kligore said with a laugh. He opened the window, extended his hand, palm up, toward the church, and blew.

The front door to Old North Church flew open, pushed by the autumn wind. The candles on the altar were instantly snuffed out. Beneath the holy cross, a web of darkness

20

floated over the altar.

Back in the Phantom, the mayor palmed a small ball of fire, no larger than a hen's egg. He casually tossed it into the air. The flame from the ball magically lit the wicks of the six candles. With the cake fiery with flames, Booboo, Ruby, and Mayor Maximus Kligore sang "Happy Birthday" to Cherry Tomato as they laughed and sped away.

Back in the church, Harry frowned as he sang. He looked at the altar with its now snuffed-out candles. Suspicion gurgled in his belly. He had sensed the approach of darkness, and now it was here. Someone had just stolen the flames from the candles. Harry was befuddled. He looked back to the front doors of the church in the direction of the Lustro's whereabouts. It was too late. The darkness had driven away.

He shook his head. Puzzled.

"It was just the wind, Harry," Mary Moon whispered.

"No, Mom," Harry whispered in reply. "It's never just the wind. Not in my world."

HARRY MOON'S UNUSUAL FATE

The white clouds chuffed through the blue autumn sky. Birds sang a merry carol in the trees, and a slight breeze carried the nutty, brown aromas of autumn. Mary Moon should have been happier that Sunday morning as she exited the double oak doors of Old North and proceeded down the stone steps of the place of worship she had grown to love.

But she was worried about Harry.

From the steps, Mary Moon watched Harry speaking to an old man at the front of the church. The old man was in rags and only stood about five feet tall. He appeared to be a beggar. No doubt, she thought, he was looking for coins that had not ended up in the offering plate.

Harry raised his voice at the poor man, and Mary did not like his tone. It was rough and demanding, almost shouting. She hurried down the steps. John Moon was behind her carrying Harvest and holding Honey's hand. They were lagging a bit, working to get everyone out of the church doors, shaking hands and greeting friends, unaware of what was happening on the sidewalk.

"Harry!" Mary Moon called out to her son as she ran down the stone steps.

"Mom, everything is okay. I've got this," Harry said looking up at her.

"What is going on?" Mary asked.

The old man cracked a nearly toothless smile. "I'm looking for a meal, my good lady." His eyes were sad and cloudy, like two pale moons.

"Mom," Harry said. "Walk away."

25

The beggar moved closer. "I'm merely asking—"

"He's not asking, Mom," Harry whispered loudly. "He's not what he seems."

"Oh, m'lady," the old man said as he looked at Mary, "I am just a poor soul from the old country who needs a meal." Mary noticed his tattered and torn shirt.

"The old country?" Harry exclaimed. "As old as hell's fire! Mom! He's not what he appears. He's here at Old North looking to snag a few new recruits for his special team!"

"Come along, Harry," Mary Moon said sharply.
"We have to hurry. The sermon ran late and we
have pancakes at Saywells at eleven. We don't
want Mr. Homer to give away our booth. Look,
your father and Honey and Harvest are already
ahead of us."

Mary opened up her purse and dug around.
She handed the beggar some loose change.

"Mom, don't," Harry said.

"Thank you, m'lady," the beggar said with
a   smile. He held the coins in his palm and
counted six quarters. She quickly grabbed
Harry's hand and dragged him down the
sidewalk.

The church bells at Old North were already
playing for the next service at eleven. Mary
shook her head, trying the best she could to
calm the cacophony of bells that were striking
inside her brain.

"Harry," Mary said softly, releasing her grip as they walked swiftly down the sidewalk and headed into town.

"Yes, Mom, I know," Harry said. "But that creature is bad news. He is an animal from hell, a monster who is masquerading as a beggar."

"People just don't understand, Harry, and you just make it worse for yourself sometimes. They don't see what you see."

21

"I know, Mom. But Oink aggravates me."

"Oink?"

"That's the hound of hell's name."

"I see," Mary said. "The noise a pig makes is the name of a beggar?"

"Yes . . . sort of," Harry said. "A beggar who is really a hound of hell."

"Okay," said Mary. "Now, I'm clear."

"Who's up for pancakes?" John Moon asked.

"Me. Me," said Harvest. "Booberries."

"Blueberries," Honey corrected.

"Booberries! Booberries!" Harvest cried.

"Okay, have it your way," Honey said.

And then she tousled Harvest's hair.

The Moon family had a wonderful time at Saywells drugstore. It had been part of the little town since World War II. It even had an old-fashioned soda counter where you could still order a hot-fudge sundae in a silver cup for ninety-six cents. Mary had been coming to Saywells since she was a little girl.

When her great-aunt Kay passed away, Kay left her house in Sleepy Hollow to Mary Moon. With Marry having just graduated from nursing college in Boston, she and John Moon were delighted to have such a lovely home for their young family to enjoy. Once they moved to Sleepy Hollow, John began commuting to Boston for work while Mary took a job as a nurse at the Sleepy Hollow Hospital.

At Saywells, the laughter of her family and the warm syrup dripping over her pancakes almost took away the pain of what Mary had just experienced with Harry. After the hearty breakfast, the family walked down Main Street toward their home on Nightingale Lane.

"Not in my world." Mary thought about what Harry had said earlier at the Old North. She was worried for her special son. "Not in my world." *What must his world look like?*

Of course, all children are special. But Harry, she had always known, had unique gifts. As she strolled home with her family, Mary turned to see Harry trailing behind, talking to what seemed to be the air as he walked down the sidewalk.

But it wasn't the air. Harry was talking to his lop-eared Harlequin friend, Rabbit. Even for a Harlequin, Rabbit was large. Rabbit had been a gift from Samson, the proprietor of the Sleepy Hollow Magic Shoppe. Rabbit was a special friend with great wisdom about the deep magic that Samson wanted Harry to learn. They made quite a pair. Of course, no one could see Rabbit except Harry unless Harry

revealed Rabbit to an audience through a magic trick.

Rabbit walked on his haunches with Harry and came up almost to Harry's waist. While Harry walked, Rabbit filled him in on the mysterious incident of the candles at Old North blowing out all at once.

"It's an ancient ritual called 'borrowing light,'" Rabbit explained. "Darkness could never make light on its own, and in ancient times, there were no lighters or matches. So darkness used its power to pull light for its own purpose."

31

Harry stopped walking and let Rabbit continue.

"You were right, Harry, when you sensed danger. Mayor Kligore blew open the front doors of the church and stole the fire. He was outside in his car and needed to light a birthday cake for one of his employees."

Harry sped up his pace. "Such a considerate boss," he said, fuming, thinking about the powerful man who had a grip over the town as strong as Iron Man.

"No doubt, that's why the mayor's assistant, Cherry Tomato, calls him 'Boss Man,'" Rabbit said.

Mary was lost in her own thoughts as she walked with her family. Absently, she listened to her husband singing "Old MacDonald Had A Farm." It was such a silly song, but the Moon children had always seemed to love it. Harry and Honey had giggled when she used to sing it to them, turning their grumpiness into gladness. Now, she could hear little Harvest laughing, hoisted high on his daddy's shoulders.

Still, Mary could not get her oldest child out of her mind. She saw his expression when he looked at her in the church this morning. Harry's frown came from his pain within, the responsibility he felt for a Sleepy Hollow in trouble.

Later that afternoon, Mary set the table for Sunday dinner. The dining room for the Moon family was really an alcove, set apart from the kitchen but still part of it.

32

As she set out the napkins and silverware for her family, Mary Moon looked around the ceiling of the alcove where a favorite saying was stenciled on the ceiling in Old New England font.

It had been stenciled there almost a hundred years ago by her great-aunt Kay, but it had faded over time.

She remembered sitting at her aunt and uncle's table when she was just a little girl. She learned the alphabet from those words. She learned grace there too.

33

The first thing that Mary and her husband did when they moved into Great-Aunt Kay's home was to restore the stenciling in the sunny alcove. Mary found the original font, and one Saturday afternoon, she and John worked a new ochre paint into the old words and restored the filigree of leaves and vines with gold leaf.

Whenever she got anxious, Mary would look at the words, and they would calm her.

She was a woman of faith, but as a working mom with three young children, Mary was often anxious. It was hard not to be.

As she set out the plates, Mary looked at the words taken from the Holy Book. She was glad she and John had restored them, for she knew that her children, as contradictory as they often were, were being raised under the guidance of a heavenly wisdom. Those words—love, joy, peace, patience, kindness, goodness, faithfulness, gentleness, and self-control—always took on meaning for her. Those words were a call to action. In the quiet before Sunday dinner, Mary fell into the calm and rest of the simple phrasing.

34

⌒ᴧ⌒

Upstairs in his bedroom, Harry was finishing a map for geology class. Harry's door was closed while he drew at his desk. Despite the DO NOT ENTER UNDER ANY CIRCUMSTANCES sign hanging on his door, Honey, ten and in fifth grade, opened the door without knocking and strolled quite deliberately into

Harry's room. Sign or no sign.

Honey was wearing a tar-black wig with bangs, black eye shadow, and a golden gown dangling with dozens of gold cardboard stars.

"Ta da!" Honey said. She paraded around Harry's desk, the stars dully thudding against the fabric of the gown. "What do you think, bro-there?" she asked.

"A little bright," Harry answered without looking up from his map homework. He was busy illustrating where the mineral and agricultural resources were located in Sleepy Hollow County.

35

"Ha! Ha! Ha! Smarty pants. Do you know who I am?" she said.

"Not a clue," he replied. Again, he did not look up.

"I ruled Egypt. I took baths in goat milk! Men died for me! Who am I?" she asked.

"Stumped," he replied with a sigh, concentrating on his map.

"That's because you get Cs in history, sweet thang. I am Cleopatra, you cretin!" she proclaimed.

"Good for you," Harry said.

"So who are you going as this Halloween, magic boy? Elvis Gold, like you always do?" she asked with a casual sigh as if she was not really interested.

"Nothin'."

"Nothin'?"

"I told Mom and Dad I would take you trick-or-treating, but I am wearing my own face this Halloween." Harry grabbed a brown colored pencil from the pile on his desk. "I'm putting away such childish things."

37

"That's no fun!" Honey stomped her foot into the carpet.

"It's what happens when you get to be in eighth grade," Harry said, breathing deeply, his chest expanding under his Do No Evil T-shirt. "You'll see when you grow up."

With a huff, Honey stomped to the door in a whirl of gold.

"Why would I grow up? I won't be Cleopatra if I grow up!" Honey said as she left the room.

She slammed the door behind her with a bang that shook Harry's desk.

"Peace at last," Harry said with a growl, trying his best to return to his project. But there was no peace for him. He was trying to finish his project, but he was also trying to understand the meaning behind the unlit candles at Old North Church.

Something was up in Sleepy Hollow. This he knew for sure. But he could not quite put his finger on it.

HIDING IN PLAIN SIGHT

Harry's night visions made him toss and turn. Even while he slept, Harry could not put the snuffing of the candles at Old North out of his head.

In a deep sleep, Harry dreamt of the citizens

of Sleepy Hollow waiting expectantly for their annual tradition to begin. The lighting of the Halloween bonfire in the town square was always the biggest celebration of the year.

At first, everyone was having a good time, eating pumpkin-spice donuts, drinking apple cider, and laughing with one another. But as the dream turned into nightmare, Harry squinted in pain. He had a sense of dread. His mind reeled in his shadowy state as he stood in the grassy square. "Something is terribly wrong!"

From the gazebo in the square, two high school seniors walked onto the sidewalk and approached the center of the green. The seniors were dressed in white ceremonial robes and wore candle wreaths upon their heads. The wreaths represented winter light and the coming of Christmas. Where the massive statue of the Headless Horseman normally stood was a tall scaffolding of autumn leaves and branches.

In his nightmare, Harry watched the entire town hush as the two festively dressed teenagers carried a hammered silver bowl of

fire toward the massive leaf pile. The flames were jumping from the bowl. When the robe-clad seniors reached the edge of the massive heap, the first student spoke.

"By this fire, we embrace the quiet of winter with the light of a new day."

With that, the two high school students turned over the silver bowl. The fire dropped onto the dry tinder, bursting into flames. The citizens of the town applauded as the fire leapt up the high scaffolding. Soon, a massive inferno flared in the very heart of the Sleepy Hollow square.

41

"Is this not the best costume ever, Harry Moon?" Honey asked, running to Harry in his nightmare. Harry had the same expression as when he witnessed the candles snuffed out at the Old North. "Look how my wig and bangles reflect the light of the bonfire!" Honey cried, twirling in her golden Cleopatra gown. The bonfire roared like a mythical beast, as frightening as the dragons torn from the pages of childhood fairy tales.

Harry looked at Honey as she stood in front of the conflagration. His nightmare had turned her into a dragon. Below her long black wig, she smiled at him from her jutting dragon jawbone. Yellow-and-orange flames jumped from her eyes.

Harry looked out at the people of Sleepy Hollow. They were all standing still as statues, mesmerized by the light of the bonfire. It was like a cast meeting for *Jurassic World*. They all wore the frightening heads of reptilian creatures inside his dreamy terror.

"Look!" Harry cried out in his sleep. "It is the curse of the bonfire! And it's hiding in plain sight!"

No one turned to him, not even his own mother and father, who, like the rest of Sleepy Hollow, had also turned into dragons!

"Nooo, Mom! Nooo, Dad!" he shouted from his deep sleep. "Turn away!"

Still concerned about Harry, Mary sat in her bed unable to sleep. John dozed next to her. Through the closed bedroom door, Mary heard the muffled shouts of her oldest son across the hall.

Mary climbed out of bed, quietly put on her robe so as not to wake her husband, opened the door to her bedroom, and crossed the hall.

"NO! Nooo!" Harry cried in his sleep. "The fire in the bowl! It was borrowed light! Where did the light come from?" He whimpered as his head turned back and forth on the pillow. "Don't trust the light!" he shouted again as Mary entered his room. "Turn away from the Halloween bonfire!"

Mary gently pressed her hand on her son's head. It was drenched in cold sweat.

"Harry, Harry," she said tenderly, sitting on the side of his mattress. "Wake up, sweetie," she said, shaking him softly.

Groggily, Harry opened his eyes. Mary Moon pulled a white cotton handkerchief from her robe pocket and mopped the perspiration from his brow.

"Sweetie, are you all right?" she asked as his eyes began to focus on her face.

Harry couldn't speak at first. But then, "Yes," he said. "I'm all right. It was just a nightmare."

Mary looked at him knowingly. "Harry, it's never just a nightmare."

Harry shook his head.

"What is it?" she asked.

"Nothing, Mom, nothing," he said. "Go back to bed."

Mary knew she would have to leave it there.

Mary understood only too well that he

simply did not want to burden her with his troubles. While she did not like it, Mary also knew that he would have to travel alone on the road of his journey. She knew she could guide him, but he was fast becoming the man he was destined to be.

She understood because of the visit from a stranger who had called upon her in the Boston Commons on the day Harry was baptized. She lingered a moment outside Harry's door. There was little she could do for Harry but to be there for him, to encourage him, to be his champion whenever possible. "I will be there, Harry," she whispered. "I will."

45

∽

The next morning, Honey was wound up as usual. At breakfast, she finished her oatmeal as quickly as she could while the rest of the family enjoyed theirs.

"I suppose you have all heard the news that Harry has shoved his Elvis Gold Halloween costume into moth balls and stuffed the box in the attic," Honey announced with a huff. "This will be the first year Harry will not be wearing a costume."

"He's still going to walk with you for trick-or-treating," John Moon replied.

"Well, I don't need Harry," said Honey to her father, imperiously holding court from her imagined throne in the alcove. "I have helpers who are going to be my gladiators. In fact, they are building a wonderful chariot for me, which I have graciously agreed to ride upon. Why wouldn't I?"

Honey swung around toward Harry and narrowed her eyes. "Do you know them, Harry? They are strong and tall guys from the sixth grade," she said as she glared across the table at her older brother, who quietly chomped on a spoonful of oatmeal with walnuts and raisins.

"Leave your brother alone," Mary warned softly.

"Why? Because he's oh-so-special?" Honey

46

shoved her bowl.

"That's right, Honey. This time, the 'do not disturb' means you," answered Mary as she placed her bowl in the sink.

"Thanks, Mom," Harry said.

John stood and dropped his napkin onto the table. "Good day, my Nightingale Knights!" he said. Since they resided on Nightingale Lane and, according to John, lived in a gorgeous castle, he had dubbed his family knights. Harry thought it was kinda cornball but got a kick out of how excited his dad was when he imagined his family as knights. John kissed Mary and all his children goodbye and hurried out the back door of the kitchen to the garage.

47

As she walked by the breakfast table, Mary gently brushed the top of Harry's head with her hand. His inky, black hair fell about his brow. His sweats were gone. And it was a brand new day. She was grateful for that.

That afternoon at the Sleepy Hollow Hospital, Mary assisted obstetrician Dr. Ricardo Mestres in delivering a baby, August Toledo, into the long line of Toledos who had lived in Sleepy Hollow for generations and generations.

Baby August was Randy Toledo's great-grandson. Randy Toledo owned the Toledo Barbershop. Harry and his dad got haircuts there. After tiny August Toledo was swaddled in a soft blue blanket and snug in his mother's arms, Mary was able to take a break. Over a cup of tea in the break room, she remembered her own pregnancy with her first born, Harry Moon.

News of Baby Harry

Mary Moon's own amazing adventure with Harry Moon began long before Harry could even talk or eat a hot-fudge sundae by himself.

It was the day she had met a most peculiar

stranger.

Outside a historic old church in Boston, John Moon held up baby Harry in his baptismal gown to the blue sky.

"One day, Harry, my boy," he said as the infant laughed at being held so high in the air, "you will be a pathfinder, creating all kinds of new innovations in Silicon Valley. I can just tell you're going to be a techie! Just like your old man."

Mary listened to her husband on the steps outside the church. "Or maybe Harry will be a doctor at Mass General," she said.

As soon as baby Harry heard his mother speak, Harry giggled just like brother Harvest would giggle in a dozen years at his own baptism at Old North in Sleepy Hollow.

Mary was practically floating on air with her son and husband around her. She loved being a mom, and she believed she would be a good one.

That afternoon, Mary pushed her sleeping infant in a baby carriage across the Boston Common. John Moon was off visiting with friends. It was John's father who had given the carriage to them as a baptism gift. The carriage was blue and gold, the colors of John's dad's old alma mater.

"Get that Moon into the sunshine every day!" William Moon had said to John about Harry. "Let him see how beautiful the world is! Keep him away from those blasted screens all the kids watch these days! Fresh air!"

Mary pushed the carriage past other families in the park. The carriage was made of sturdy, dark-blue canvas. Mary loved taking Harry for fresh-air walks. As she strolled through the park, a sweet little fountain captured her eye. It was a bronze sculpture of a child sitting on a pile of rocks playing with the water. The sculpture, known as the Small Child Fountain, was cracked with age, adding to its quaint and timeless charm. Mary pushed the carriage closer. Harry laughed as its wheels bounced along the cobblestones surrounding the fountain. Mary laughed with him.

It was just after she had stopped to observe the sweet sculpture that something strange and wonderful happened. This was the seemingly innocent event that would change Mary forever.

A man in a purple cape and red slippers walked up to the fountain. He scooped up water from the seashell basin with his hands and started washing his face with the bubbling water.

Mary Moon could not help but stare at the man.

But, just as she had been attracted to the fountain, she felt drawn to the peculiar man.

At first, she thought the stranger was homeless, but she quickly changed her mind. His purple cape, while odd, didn't seem to bear much wear or soil. Indeed, it was pristine. And his red slippers seemed new.

The man turned to her. "I figured if the water is fresh enough for this baby, Mary," he said as he pointed to the sculpture of the child, "it's fresh enough for me."

Mary felt her heart quicken. "How do you know my name?" she asked.

The man shrugged. "I just know things."

He splashed more water on his face. Mary stood perfectly still, watching and waiting for something to happen next. Nothing did, and yet, she still stood there.

"Something wrong?" The man stood. He flicked water playfully at her with his fingers. She blinked, recoiling as the drops hit her face and shoulders. He laughed, his periwinkle eyes twinkling. "Something right, then?" he asked.

Mary, never at a loss for words, was suddenly speechless.

"Not accustomed to entertaining angels, are we?" he asked.

Mary gasped. "Is . . . is that what you are?"

"Maybe, he said with a wink. "Not . . . necessarily. But, maybe."

"A magician, then?" she asked. "Is that how you know my name? With the cape, I thought that maybe . . ."

"Well, we are all magicians, Mary Moon. We all have the deep magic within us. Except most of us never learn that."

54

"What is it that you want from me?" she asked.

"I don't want anything from you," he replied, somewhat startled by her question.

"You must want something," she said.

"Quite the opposite. I have something for you, Mary Moon."

Mary swallowed. "You do? But . . . What—"

"Let me break it to you gently. Harry is not going to be working at Google in Silicon Valley."

"How do you know my son's name?"

"Nor Is he going to be a doctor at Mass General or in Kalamazoo or Timbuktu, for that matter," the stranger said.

Mary couldn't help but feel just a little nervous. But yet, she knew she didn't want to run away either. "Who are you?"

55

Then he hesitated for a moment. "That is, he won't be either of those things if you are a good mother to him."

"Of course I will be a good mother," she said, never taking her eyes off the stranger with the red slippers and a face beaded with water.

"Good," he said, nodding. "Then, as his mom, you must guide Harry to who he is destined to be, not who you and John want him to be."

He reached into the baby carriage. "I have washed my hands, so not to worry," he said.

"Hey, wait a minute! Stop! Put Harry down!" she shouted.

He turned and stared at her. His eyes revealed grace of such power that she knew he meant no harm. There was no darkness in his eyes. There was nothing but softness.

"Do not fear, dear one," the cloaked stranger said to Mary as he lifted Harry out of the carriage.

"Who are you?"

"Fate goes as fate must," he replied.

"Is that from the Holy Book?"

"Beowulf," he answered.

The old man held Harry Moon up before him

and laughed with wonder at the baby. Harry giggled at the sight of the man's face and twinkling periwinkle eyes.

"Oh, you are a pudgy one, aren't you?" the man said. Then the stranger turned his

57

attention to Mary. "To be a good mother, Mary Moon, you must stop believing that you are going to write this child's book. You must understand that the only thing for you to do, as the good mother you were meant to be, is to help turn the pages of his story with love and with wisdom."

Mary could not help but notice how calm Harry was in the stranger's arms. He cooed and gurgled with delight. "I only want to do what is right for him," Mary softly said.

"All children are special, Mary. Harry will be very different from your second child, Honey, or your third child, Harvest. And all of them, I assure you, will be special human beings. But Harry is different."

"I will have three children?" Mary asked, watching the man with her baby.

The man smiled. "Harry is unique, for he was born with a special gift of sight, with eyes able to see things that are unseen. He has talents to move matter by the sound of his voice."

The man stopped and looked into Mary's eyes to see if she was keeping up. "Pretty amazing, huh?

"He will need to develop a soft heart and a will that holds goodness," he said. " He must learn this from you and the way your wise and loving hand turns the pages of his story. That is how he will come to know good when he is older—by the way your hand lovingly turns the pages of his story."

The man lay Harry back into the carriage and tucked his warm blue blanket around him. "I will send someone to help him with his gifts, to help him become the Harry he is meant to be."

59

"You will send him someone?"

"Yes," the eccentrically dressed man replied.

"How will I know this one you are sending?" Mary asked.

"Oh, you will know. You can't miss him," he replied with a soft laugh. "His ears are huge. The left one dangles a bit."

"What will Harry become, then?" Mary asked.

"What all boys and girls are destined to become if they simply believe."

Mary looked questioningly at the stranger with the periwinkle eyes.

"They become magic," he said with a smile.

Mary looked at him and somehow knew. "But he will have more magic than most?"

60 "Just turn the pages, Mary Moon," said the man, a stranger no longer. "One day at a time. Be ready for each morning, each new page. Such is the way of fate. The Prince of the Air may rule the world, but last I checked the Great Magician still owns the place. Peace, my dearest Mary. We will meet again in Sleepy Hollow."

"Sleepy Hollow?" Mary Moon asked.

"At the house of your great-aunt Kay. You have such wonderful memories of that house, don't you, Mary?"

"I do have fond memories. But how do you

know?"

"I see it in your eyes. Just as I see the wonder of your child."

Mary pondered the wisdom and the treasure of the man. He softly said, "Goodbye." His twinkling periwinkle eyes seemed to float in the Sunday afternoon air. Then, he was gone.

Mary blinked back tears remembering that meeting with the man in the Boston Commons.

61

Driving home from work in her blue electric car, she could not get Harry out of her mind. It was raining. Through the splattered windshield, the streets of her little town seemed empty of people, which suddenly made her feelings cold and desperate.

From Main Street, Mary turned onto Mt. Sinai Road. As the autumn wind blew, she parked her car and ran up the sidewalk to Old North Church. It was storming hard by then. She dashed as quickly as her feet would take her, splashing through the puddles in the driving rain. Mary pushed open the double oak doors and passed across the threshold of the church.

Old North was empty. It was dark but for the candles in lanterns at the altar. She wondered if the candles had been placed in lantern glass because of the incident the other day. "It's never just the wind," her son had said.

Mary called out into the church. "Just tell me, Rabbit! Is Harry going to be all right?!" Mary was beside herself. She was always so together. She lived an orderly and peaceful life. She collapsed in the front pew, falling to her knees.

She brushed a tear from her cheek.

"I can't help it! I worry, that's all. I don't know what he is going through. There is no magician's playbook to turn the pages! I can't compare. I can't know. And he won't tell me about his nightmares because he's trying to be a man. But he is only thirteen, Rabbit! He is still my little one, isn't he? Just please tell me, Rabbit, is Harry going to be okay!"

Shouting into the empty church calmed her. She settled down. Her rapid breathing slowed. She moved off her knees and sat quietly in the front-row pew, in front of the altar.

In the sound that lives beyond the silence, Mary Moon heard a faint voice. "He's going to be fine." As soon as she heard the whisper, she stood.

63

"Rabbit is that you? Are you here, Rabbit?" she called out into the darkness. There was no answer. She sat on the pew bench, speaking quietly to herself. She looked out at the many burning lanterns around the altar.

"What does he have that others do not? He looks at me so strangely, Rabbit," she said softly. "So often, I think I hardly know my own son."

"It is difficult to understand the journey of a hero," the whisperer said.

She thought for a moment that the voice certainly sounded like Rabbit. From time to time she had heard the voice when Harry was speaking to his invisible friend. Or at least, invisible to her and everyone else.

"There are things that Harry must go through," the whisperer continued.

64

"What things?" She asked.

The whisperer replied, "Growing pains."

CRAZY GENIUS

Mary, Honey, and Harry Moon attended the high school production of George Bernard Shaw's classic play *Saint Joan* at Sleepy Hollow High School. Harry's former babysitter and love crush, Sarah Sinclair, seventeen and a junior at the high school, played the lead—Joan of Arc.

In his auditorium seat, Harry was all eyes as he watched the stage. He thought Sarah was the most beautiful girl in the whole wide world. Like any teenager, Sarah made a lot of mistakes, especially in handling Harry's feelings for her. As far as Harry was concerned, Sarah Sinclair could do no wrong.

"She is so good in this, don't you think?" he whispered.

"Just fabulous," Honey Moon replied.

"I was asking Mom," Harry said.

"Fabulous," Mary said.

On stage, the pretty Sarah Sinclair, in a simple white tunic and shaved wig, knelt before the judge, a French magistrate.

"I love the Church but not the English!" Sarah said as Joan of Arc. "They will not yield to prayers! They understand nothing but hard knocks and slashes."

The judge came closer to the penitent Sarah. He bent his face to her, glowering with his beady eyes. "But who tells you to do these acts, Joan?"

"I hear voices telling me what to do," she replied softly. "The voices come from God."

"God?" he said with disdain. "They come from your imagination!"

"Of course. That is how the messages of God come to us!"

67

Harry listened carefully and nodded, for indeed he heard Rabbit all the time, advising him, educating him, correcting him, encouraging him. But he knew that his mom struggled to understand where the voice came from.

"Do you feel better now?" Harry asked, leaning into his mom. "Who does that remind you of? The voices?"

Honey sat on the other side of Mary but had no problem answering for her mother.

"Why should I feel better? I'm not sick."

"I do feel better, Harry," Mary said as she squeezed her son's hand. "But we must remember to test those voices. We must make sure that when the voices come, they are from the light, not the dark."

"Yes, I sometimes forget to test, Mom," Harry whispered.

"Just remember to ask, 'Do you serve the Great Magician?' If the voices answer, 'Yes,' then trust the voices. If they do not, don't listen to them. If you have a Good Mischief Team, Harry, you guys better be sure you are fighting for the right side!" she said softly and with a smile.

The curtain closed on the play. Terry Toledo, the high school drama teacher and aunt to the new August Toledo Jr., came onto the stage. She beamed like a bright morning sun for her thespians. With exuberance, Mrs. Toledo addressed the packed auditorium.

"Joan of Arc believed that her ideas came

from a heavenly source. Was she crazy? Was she a genius? George Bernard Shaw, the author of this play, says only this: 'Joan of Arc was burned at the stake by those who feared her. Two centuries later, she was canonized Saint Joan by those who loved her.' He wants you to decide the point of view."

After Mrs. Toledo had finished talking, the curtain opened. One by one, and to great applause, the cast assembled at the front of the stage.

69

Finally, in full steel armor, her red-pink hair shining, Sarah Sinclair appeared for her curtain call. Harry's heart jumped into his throat. She looked so awesome in her shining silver breastplate.

"Now, that's a Nightingale Knight," said Harry.

"Except she doesn't live on Nightingale Lane," whispered Honey.

"One day she will," Harry said.

"Eewww, gross," Honey said as her eyebrows arched.

As the applause continued, the audience gave her a standing ovation. Of course, the Moon clan was first to be on their feet.

"Fabulous!" Honey shouted.

70

For once, Harry Moon begrudgingly agreed with his sister.

"I'll second that 'fabulous,'" said Harry.

"Hashtag fabulous," Honey said as she snapped a picture of Sarah with her phone.

She thumbed a quick text. "Soon the world will know how fabulous your former babysitter is." She looked at Harry. "And of course," she said, "your future wife. NOT!"

Since it was still warm for an autumn night, Harry and his mom and sister walked home from the high school. Their house on Nightingale Lane was only a few blocks away. Ever since John Moon's father had bought her family a baby carriage for their "fresh air" strolls, Mary always made it a point to walk with her family in their small town whenever they could.

"Mom, you don't think I'm nuts, do you?" Harry asked.

71

"I do, Harry, I really do," Honey answered. "And because we believe, Harry, that your voices are *not* real, we look forward to the day you, yourself, might burn at the stake!"

"I was talking to Mom, stupid!" Harry said, lashing out at Honey.

"That's right, Honey, calm down now," Mary said taking her daughter's hand and shaking it gently. "And please do not call your sister stupid."

Harry walked quietly behind them.

"You know, Harry," Mary said, "you are always talking about checking your gut. That's where I think, if we really listen carefully, we can hear God. So no, I do not think you are crazy for hearing Rabbit's voice. And yes, I believe you are quite special."

"Mom, don't encourage him!" Honey said, stomping her feet as she walked.

"That's what moms do, Honey. We encourage

our children when they are in the right," Mary Moon replied.

"The RIGHT?" Honey said, flipping out. "Oh mother, that is just so *wrong!*"

74

THE INK STORM

A fter school the next day, Harry walked through the town square to the offices of the local paper, *Awake In Sleepy Hollow*. Even though it had rained hard for a short while the night before, Harry saw that there were still a lot of leaves to fall from the giant oaks and elms in the grassy center of the town. Preparation activity was high in the square for Halloween the next day. Of course, this was Spooky Town, where every day was Halloween night.

Pine scaffolding was constructed around the Headless Horseman statue, the main tourist attraction of the town. Truckloads of branches and leaves from the community neighborhoods were being hauled into the square for the traditional Halloween bonfire.

The food establishments were raising their booths and tents. Wooden stands were erected for apple cider, the famous donut dunk, and the hot pea soup, courtesy of the Haunted Wood Brasserie. The festive energy was pitched high. Harry even snagged a free cinnamon elephant ear from Adele Cracken, who worked at Saywells.

Harry walked up the steps and through the single door of the tiny editorial offices of the town's newspaper. There he found Mrs. Mildred Middlemarch, the white-haired editor in chief of the local paper. Harry requested entry into the archives. He told her he wanted to read about the day when "everything changed."

"What do you mean, Harry?" the stout and friendly Mrs. Middlemarch asked.

"The day when the fortunes turned for Sleepy Hollow, the day we became Spooky Town, when every day became Halloween night."

"When the Headless Horseman statue first arrived in the green?" she asked.

"That would be it, Mrs. Middlemarch."

"Come with me," she said.

Harry followed her down a long wooden hallway in the old building constructed some two hundred years ago. She opened a door, distressed from over two centuries of wear and tear.

Mrs. Middlemarch sighed deeply. "Can you imagine how wonderful it would be to have all

that history available at the click of a mouse?"
She paused. "But convincing the board is . . .
well, let's just leave it that."

"You mean We Drive By Night, the company
that owns the paper, has not approved the
budget for digital archives?" Harry asked.

"That would be correct, Harry," she said with
an ironic lilt to her voice.

When they reached the dark repository
room in the basement of the old building, Mrs.
Middlemarch again apologized for the sorry
surroundings.

Harry Moon frowned at the room. It was
pitiful. Beneath a single light bulb that hung
from a beam, a lone library table stood in the
middle of the room. Dark gray file cabinets
surrounded the perimeter of the table. It looked
like the cabinets hadn't been dusted in years.

"I'm sorry, Harry," said Mrs. Middlemarch
as she opened a file cabinet labeled with the
year that interested Harry. "The ink used for

the early newspapers was cheap and most of the articles have faded. Some stories have disappeared completely from the pages."

"It figures that the mayor, who just happens to own the paper of this town, purchases cheap ink to record its history," replied Harry.

"Some think it was deliberate," Mrs. Middlemarch whispered.

19

Mrs. Mildred Middlemarch was between a rock and a hard place. Harry knew it. She worked for Mayor Maximus Kligore, but she did not trust him.

"Of course the disappearing ink is intentional," Harry said. "That way, the mayor controls the story of Sleepy Hollow. If there is no history, it's easy to fill citizens with false versions of their past. What I want to get to, Mrs. Middlemarch, is the story of that first Halloween bonfire."

"That much I do know," said Mrs.

Middlemarch. "I don't need a faded paper to tell you that." She sat down at the table.

"The tradition started around the time my husband and I moved here," she said. "That was fifteen years ago. It was the night the selectmen revealed the arrival of the Headless Horseman statue in the square. For many years, the annual Halloween bonfire was held in Melville Field. But that year, the mayor moved the bonfire to the square to coincide with the unveiling of the statue." With a paper towel, Mrs. Middlemarch wiped dust from the table.

"We all thought it was strange to move the bonfire," she continued. "Even I, who was new to the town and had been hired to run the paper, thought it was weird. Of course, the fire department was concerned about the tall maples and elms in the square catching fire. But the selectmen thought the townies wanted a big show for the unveiling of the statue and were prepared to take the risk."

Mrs. Middlemarch spread the faded papers

on the table while Harry took a seat.

"All the leaves and fall debris were loaded into the center of town. The bonfire heap was so tall that it hid the statue. Once the bonfire was lit, the fire illuminated the entire square with light. As the fire drew down, the flames parted like a curtain on a stage. Through the flames, for everyone to witness, was the great stallion and his headless rider."

"Didn't you find that creepy, Mrs. Middlemarch? It's like a headless horseman from Hell!" Harry asked in the dark basement.

"Harry, don't you think the mayor wanted it be a little creepy? It was Halloween, after all," Mrs. Middlemarch replied.

Mrs. Middlemarch rose from the table and said goodbye, leaving Harry to his archives. The vast room was dark and rather spooky, but Harry hunkered down at the table and began looking through the old newspapers that Mrs. Middlemarch had laid out for him. As he scanned them, he found that the papers were almost blank from the faded ink. Harry wondered if this really was cheap ink or was it a trick by the mayor to keep the truth concealed?

After rustling through the faded papers, Harry pulled his wand from his back pocket. He thrust it up into the air. As he waved the wand with his right hand, he softly said the word that garnered great power. Harry Moon had much to learn on his magical adventure. His teacher of magic had not filled him in on the full meaning of the word. Harry only knew that he needed to speak the word with both confidence and reverence.

"A B R A C A D A B R A," proclaimed Harry.

With the utterance of the word and the thrusting of the wand to pierce the air, the nature of the dingy room changed. The single bulb over Harry's head that shone on the table blinked at his voice to become many bulbs. Now, he could actually see how badly the articles from fifteen years ago had faded.

"You know what I think, Rabbit?" Harry said, as he looked at the faded front page of the Halloween edition of *Awake*.

"What do you think, Harry, my friend?" Rabbit replied.

Whenever Harry asked for Rabbit, he was almost always there. Rabbit was sitting now in the chair that Mrs. Middlemarch had occupied just a few minutes ago. Rabbit blew on the table, clearing a section of it so that he could crook his furry black-and-white elbow. He rested his black-and-white head easily in his paw.

"I don't think this is cheap ink at all," Harry said. "There is not enough variant in this." He held up the front page of one of the issues. "A normal aged page would have erratic marks and yellowing. But all these pages are exactly the same in their aging."

"Then what is it, boy genius?" Rabbit asked.

"Black magic," Harry replied.

Once again, Harry thrust his wand toward the ceiling while Rabbit watched. This was the same kind of wood that was used in Aaron's rod in the ancient story, which sprouted almond nuts every season, turned river water to blood, and made the sea wide so that the Hebrews could cross through it.

"Ink come near!" Harry commanded. "Ink adhere to what was dear. Truth survives in the story of our lives. A B R A C A D A B R A."

From the ceiling beams, there was a rumble, like thunder. Then a flash from the multitude of bulbs, like lightning. Black ink rained from the ceiling.

Rabbit and Harry watched as the black liquid squirted over the file cabinets and poured into drawers and shelves, streaking over the archive table. Harry held up a paper with a banner that he could now read clearly:

Sleepy Hollow Begins a New Act

Headless Horseman Statue Revealed Through Bonfire's Curtain of Flames

By Mildred Middlemarch

Harry feverishly read the article as Rabbit sat beside him.

"Mrs. Middlemarch is a pretty good writer," said Rabbit.

"For sure," Harry said, scouring the paper for any clue he could hold onto. He read past the front page and turned to page eight. This page was also completely legible as a result of the ink storm, which, when it ended, left the room spotless and the paper loaded with readable black print.

"Look, Rabbit, Mrs. Middlemarch was thorough. Here's the quote from someone at the bonfire."

"What does it say?" Rabbit asked, squinting at page eight. "My magic only goes so far. I can see through walls and into time, but I hang it up when I get to the small print."

"Okay, listen carefully," Harry said. "Here's the quote from the guy who appears to have borrowed the silver bowl of fire to start the bonfire. Okay?"

Rabbit lifted his lop ears into the air, holding one in each paw. Harry had to laugh when he saw those two big ears extended straight up.

"As you can see," said Rabbit, "I am all ears . . . literally."

"'By this fire, we embrace the quiet of winter with the light of a new day,'" Harry read.

"I don't get it," Rabbit said. "So they are ushering in Christmas?"

"Of course you get it. What light are they referring to?"

"The light of the Christmas child?"

"Not at all! That's just what they want you to believe."

"Really? Why don't they just say what they mean?" asked Rabbit, still stretching his ears toward the ceiling.

"Because it's a sleight of hand. What are

they really doing here? Evil is hiding in plain sight. This is not the light of Christmas that takes us through the winter. This is the fire of hell meant to enchant us! I think these poor unsuspecting high school seniors in those advent costumes at the Halloween bonfire are just fools and tools."

"Seniors are tools?" Rabbit said incredulously.

"Knock it off, Rabbit. Listen, they are not calling for the light of Christmas. They are calling for Sleepy Hollow to be visited by darkness!"

"Holy moly!" shouted Rabbit, so excited that he dropped his ears and shook his head in amazement.

Of course, Rabbit really knew what was going on. But a friend such as Rabbit is an encourager, a prompter toward truth, not necessarily the guy who gives the answer. All humans must find their own answers on the highway of their lives.

"So what do you think, Harry?" asked Rabbit.

"This is some kind of curse?"

"Rabbit, it sure as heck is not some kind of blessing!"

From behind the darkness of the file cabinets, Harry and Rabbit heard: "Dum de dum dum."

"Is somebody there?" Harry called out to the darkness. He grabbed his wand in case he needed to protect himself and Rabbit.

"Dum de dum dum dum."

Now it was Harry's turn to squint, for he could not see anything in the darkness. He saw movement in the gloom, and then, there before him, appeared the silhouette of a man in shadow.

"Looks like you found some neat stuff, huh?" the voice said. "Dum de dum dum dum."

90

FROM THE SHADOWS

"Maybe. Kinda neat," Harry said, apprehensively, straining his eyes into the darkness. "Who are you, anyways?" Harry threw his voice into the shadows.

"I'm Abraham," answered the figure.

"Interesting name," Harry said.

"I'm the night watchman. I work for Old Lady Middlemarch."

"Oh really?" Harry asked.

"Really," said the watchman.

"It's kinda dusty and dirty around here for someone who's here every night," Harry said.

"I told you, I'm the night watchman. Not the cleaning lady. I don't do dust. Dum de dum dum dum."

"Where have I heard that song?"

"Maybe in your nightmares. I like to watch those too."

"Oh really?"

"Really."

Harry took a long look at the creature

standing before him. His legs appeared strong but thin. He had a large middle and a hunched back. His neck was thick and short, and his head was big with pricked-up ears like an animal.

"Mind if I ask you what might seem a random question?"

"Fire away, son," replied the figure.

"Do you believe in the Great Magician?" Harry asked.

The figure chortled. "That is a random question!"

"Answer it, spirit!" Harry said.

"Spirit? I'm the night watchman!"

"Who happens to watch my nightmares too? You're no night watchman! You're an EVIL beast sent from the dark bowels of the supernatural! You are masquerading as a watchman who calls himself Abraham," Harry proclaimed.

"But you are really a bulldog from hell! Show yourself, Oink, for you will not acknowledge the deep magic!"

Harry turned his wand to the dark shadows behind the figure.

The figure only chuckled.

"It must be those fumes from your magic ink that you've been inhaling," the figure said. "Because you are one crazy boy, Harry Moon. Talking about hell. Why, there is no hell!"

"Oh really?" Harry said.

"Really," replied the watchman. His hunched back loomed in the shadows.

"I think you are wrong, demon!" said Harry as the wand flared with light, now exposing the corner of the archive room.

There in front of Harry and Rabbit stood the ugliest creature anyone could ever imagine, upright on his haunches and dressed in a blue security uniform. It was Oink, the dreaded hound from Folly Farm, one of the many dark characters from the We Drive By Night Company.

"They say you have the sight, but you don't have any sight," said the impossibly ugly dog to Harry. "I'm just a security guard doing his job to make sure no secret sauce is stolen." The demon took his left paw and adjusted his lapel so that his gold badge could be seen clearly by Harry.

95

It read: We Drive By Night.

"How you go on about hell, Harry Moon," said the dog "You and I both know there is no hell."

"Oh, there is a hell all right, Oink!" Harry said as he stood, exposing Rabbit sitting behind him. "But it is clearly sad and lame if you happen to be the hound guarding it,"

The ugly hound bared his fangs, snarling when he saw Rabbit.

"Leave me alone. I'm just a little rabbit, that's all I am," Rabbit said, turning away from the huge ugly hound.

Harry dropped the articles he was reading in the re-file box.

"Got you moving, didn't I, wiz boy?" Oink growled. He dropped onto all fours. The hound bared his fangs wider still. His gums were blood drenched. He glowered at Harry and Rabbit.

"In your dreams," Harry replied as he walked out of the room. With a twitch of his wand, Harry plunged the room back into darkness.

BaaaaaRNGGG! The room vibrated with the sound of Oink bumping his huge head into the file cabinets by the stairs.

∽

When she looked up from her desk, all Mildred Middlemarch could see was Harry climbing the stairs. She did not see Rabbit. "Find what you needed, Harry?" she asked.

"I did. Thanks for your help. By the way, I put the articles in the re-file box, and I figured out a way to get the ink back on the pages."

"What? How did you do that?"

"How I always do it, Mrs. Middlemarch. I relied on the magic of the Great Magician."

"You are a marvel," she said with a smile.

"I'm not the marvel, the Great Magician is," Harry said as he waved his wand high as if leading a parade, exiting the editorial offices of *Awake In Sleepy Hollow*.

As he walked down the steps from the offices of the newspaper, Harry turned to Rabbit. "What was all that down there?"

"What was all what?" Rabbit asked demurely.

"You know," Harry said. Then he spoke in a weak, fearful voice and twirled his hands in the air. "I'm just an itty-bitty rabbit, that's all

97

I am!"

"I just like messin' with him, that's all."

"One day, he's gonna mess with you for good."

"Oh yeah?" said Rabbit. "Right now, he just gets a whiff of me. Wait until he tastes me."

Harry smiled and shook his head. He didn't always understand Rabbit, but he sure did like having him around.

The massive red-brick Clock Tower in the town square struck every hour for all Sleepy Hollow to hear. The tower stood two stories tall. Harry crossed the Sleepy Hollow square toward the town's fire station. He tapped on his phone.

"Mom," he commanded the phone. In a moment, his mom answered.

"Hi, Harry," Mary Moon said. "Do you have me on speaker?"

"Yes, I just wanted the whole world to know I love my mom," he said cheerily against the dark, chilly night.

"Stop buttering me up. What's the deal?" she asked.

"There's no deal," he said. He took the phone off speaker and held it to his ear. "I just wanted to let you know I will be home by curfew."

"Okay," his mom said. "Where are you?"

"I was doing some research at the newspaper, and now I'm headed to finish it up with Chief Mike at the fire station."

"Harry?"

"Huh?"

"I love you too," said Mary. "And you know what?"

"What?"

"It's not important that the whole world knows I love you. I just need you to know."

"I know," he said, slouching his shoulders, disconnecting the cell.

As hard as he was trying to become a man, Harry was touched by his mom. She was always there for him, just as Rabbit was always there for him.

100

On Nightingale Lane, Mary hung up the phone in the kitchen and smiled.

"Nice job," a voice said.

"Nice job?" Mary replied.

The voice was familiar. She could not be certain, but she thought it was the voice of Samson Dupree.

"Nice job of turning the pages," the voice said.

"Well, I'm either a genius," Mary said, "or I am crazy." She thought of the play of Saint Joan. *Was Joan of Arc crazy or did she hear voices of the divine?*

"You're not crazy, Mary Moon," the voice replied.

As he walked to the fire station, Harry passed the scaffolding being constructed around the statue for the Halloween bonfire. He looked through the wood grid and spied the severed head in the rider's arms. For a moment, Harry thought he saw Oink on its face, slyly winking at him.

Harry entered the fire station and looked up at the deputy chief's desk in the lobby where he acted as receptionist. The lobby, painted in a dreary eggshell, needed a refresher coat.

"Can I help you?" asked the sour-faced deputy.

"Yeah, I want to see Chief Mike." Harry sneered. Surprisingly, Harry's tone was sharp and rude. This was not like Harry, who always seemed courteous to everyone.

"Let's start with me. How can I help you, young man?" growled the deputy.

"You can help me by getting out of my way, Oink," Harry said in a loud, strong voice.

102

Harry breezed right past the ugly hound, now dressed in way-too-big fire battalion gear. Harry headed down the corridor.

∞

"Who is this Oink that Moon keeps referring to?" Oink asked himself as he looked at his reflection in a window. He thought he looked quite dashing in his battalion garb. Harry Moon seemed to be the only human being in the whole wide universe who could spot his disguises, who could see him hiding in plain sight.

"I have to work harder at this," Oink said, shaking his head with a growl. "When I look at my reflection, I don't see Oink. How does Harry Moon see Oink?"

Harry walked to the back office of the fire chief, Mike Orize. Mike was at his desk talking to a local on the phone. He waved Harry into his office. As with anyone in this small town, Mike and Harry knew each other well.

103

Mike treated Harry like an adult, and Harry very much liked that because, while he was only thirteen, as far as he was concerned, he was an adult.

Once Chief Mike hung up the phone, the two guys got down to the core of the issue relating to the Halloween bonfire.

"The Halloween bonfire is like a private party, isn't it?" Chief Mike told Harry.

Chief Mike explained that the roads

entering Sleepy Hollow were blocked to tourism after six p.m. on Halloween night. No one was allowed to enter the town from any of the surrounding roads without a transfer sticker on their car. A transfer sticker gave a Sleepy Hollow resident access to the town dump to transfer their garbage, and it also gave them a pass to enter Sleepy Hollow on Halloween night.

"I guess it is a private party. It's one of the few I get invited to," said Harry.

"The only vehicles that are allowed access are the fire trucks from Cambridge and Boston," said the chief. "They are our boost-strength if the bonfire should ever get out of control. We added those trucks when the bonfire was moved into town."

"So the only people allowed in the town on Halloween night are the citizens of Sleepy Hollow?" asked Harry.

"That would be the private party," said Chief Mike, nodding.

"How long has this been going on?" Harry asked.

"Since the night everything changed."

"Hey," said Harry, "I used those same words."

"Well, it's the truth. It happened the night the Headless Horseman was unveiled."

Munching on a hot dog in the Sleepy Hollow Middle School cafeteria the next day, Harry Moon explained his theory to his pals at lunch. He sat with Declan, Bailey, and Hao. It was Hot Dog Thursday.

"Are you telling us that the bonfire is really a doorway?" asked Hao.

"Not a doorway but an enchanted wall. That's how the mayor and the selectmen keep control over our little town. Every year, they make the unsuspecting citizens reaffirm their vow to pledge allegiance to Spooky Town under the spell of the fire," answered Harry.

"Rad!" replied Declan.

"Even the kids. That's why curfew for trick-or-treating ends at eight p.m.—so all the kids can be there for the curse oath by eight fifteen," said Harry.

"But it's just a theory," said Bailey, his brow furrowed in tension. "You don't know for sure that this enchanted fire is a fact. Do you Harry Moon?"

Harry pushed back his seat a bit from his empty plate. "Not totally for sure." He sighed, feeling a bit discouraged.

"How you going to know for sure?" asked Declan, glancing at his Apple watch. "The bonfire starts in seven and a half hours."

"Good point, Declan. I have to get proof. I can't go off my rocker in front of a whole town tonight. But I think I know how I can be certain," Harry said.

"How?" asked Hao.

"I have to pay a visit to the Sleepy Hollow Magic Shoppe."

108

IMPENETRABLE

O n the town's Magic Row, Harry Moon passed all the Spooky Town shops until he reached the Sleepy Hollow Magic Shoppe. For the last several years, ever since he had the itch for magic, Harry Moon had been a regular customer of the shop with the bright yellow-and-red-striped awning.

As the door opened, he was greeted by the tinkling brass bell that hung from the door hinge. It was like a welcome mat of sweet noise for Harry.

The eccentric proprietor of the store greeted Harry Moon. He wore a plastic, gold crown, ruby slippers, and a purple cape. He was the strange man who had visited Mary Moon in the Boston Common over thirteen years ago.

"Hullo, Samson."

"Hi, Harry. How are you doing, my friend?" the man asked.

"Better now for seeing you, Samson."

"Well, that makes my day." Samson smiled beneath his plastic crown.

The store was bright and sunny. It seemed there were an infinite amount of tricks and games in the ordered and brightly lit shop. It was a general store for any budding young wizard who was serious about magic. The store was loaded with books on magic. Even though there were dozens of kids in the small store, Samson gave Harry his complete attention. Samson was that kind of proprietor—where everyone felt special when they entered the door.

Harry thought it is was heaven on earth.

"Samson, I know you are busy, but do you have five minutes to lend me an ear?"

111

"You can have both of them, Harry Moon," Samson said with a bright, warm smile. He looked around the bustling store and the busy check-out counter and saw that all was buzzing in a very healthy fashion.

"Why don't we go outside so we can talk?" Samson said, as he put his hand on Harry's shoulder. "My secret helpers can run things fine without me for a few minutes."

"Your secret helpers?" Harry asked.

Samson only smiled in reply. There was

much about magic that Harry Moon still needed to understand.

They walked outside the store onto Magic Row. The magic shop looked out onto the square. The streets were bustling with activity and last-minute shopping for the big Halloween night.

"So you know why I'm here?" Harry asked, looking up at the old man.

112

"Why do you ask *that?*" Samson laughed as he adjusted his gold crown on his stack of black hair.

"How long have I been coming here, Samson?" asked Harry.

"I don't know. What would you figure?"

"Seems like forever."

"Why, that sounds like a sure bet," Samson said as he scratched his chin in thoughtful consideration.

"And in all that time, have you *ever* suggested we step outside?" Harry asked.

"Why, I don't believe I have."

"No, you haven't, kind sir," Harry said, with a grin. "So my best guess is that you know why I'm here and that outside is the perfect place to have a conversation about what's in front of our very eyes." Harry's eyes narrowed. "The scaffolding for the bonfire."

"That's not why I brought you out here," Samson said. "Let's walk."

113

They walked across the sidewalk and to the median of the curb. Parked in front of the shop was Mayor Kligore's shiny black Phantom Lustro car, and soaring atop it was the lovely golden hood ornament.

"You know, the problem with this hood ornament is not the gold itself," Samson said. He reached out and put his hands on the winged figure. "This golden sculpture is pretty, don't you think?"

"Yes," Harry replied with a shrug.

"The problem, Harry, is when we want gold too much, at the expense of other things. If we are not very careful, we can follow this desire with our whole heart and end up chasing the winged being down the wrong road.

"There is nothing wrong with making Sleepy Hollow a destination for commerce or gold, for that matter, but not at the expense of our hearts. The heart, Harry, is wonderful. But if it is not nurtured by reason and self-control, it can grow dark. It can deceive and destroy us."

114

"So is that what's really behind the bonfire? Getting rich?" said Harry.

Samson looked at Harry. "When the accumulation of wealth is the most important objective of life, it can only bring ruin in the end."

Harry listened carefully to what Samson had to say. Scratching an itch on his nose, Harry looked out at the town green before them.

"Was it reasonable to ask good people to change their businesses and celebrate Halloween year round so that they could feed their families, grow their homes, and have a comfortable life together?" asked Samson.

"I guess so," said Harry.

"Then do you think it is also reasonable to take away the good people's will, to enchant them, using magic to have them believe things that are not true?"

"No, absolutely not," replied Harry.

"Why not?" asked Samson.

"Well, it is what you have taught me, Samson. Our ability to choose is sacred. It's what makes humans special," Harry said. "Everyone has a right to make their own choices. The people of Sleepy Hollow deserve the chance to choose."

"So, Harry, you have to decide if you believe the bonfire enchantment is right or wrong for the people of the town. And if it's wrong, what you are going to do about it?"

A darkness fell across the hood of the car. The shadow drifted over Samson and Harry as they chatted. A chill shivered up Harry Moon's spine.

"Get away from my Phantom, old man!" said an angry voice.

116 The boy turned to see Mayor Kligore and his attractive entourage of women standing at the curb. They had been at the town green supervising last-minute details for the night's big events.

Cherry Tomato sneered as she grabbed Samson's wrist and pried his fingers from the golden Flying Lady hood ornament.

"He has a name, and it is Samson!" said Harry, defending his friend against the powerful mayor. Samson stepped back from the car.

"Do you know how much this car is worth?"

said the mayor. But he was not really interested in anyone's answer but his own. "It's worth four hundred and twenty-five thousand dollars, folks, that's how much. That's a lot of magic wands, old man."

The mayor Jumped into the front passenger seat while Booboo Hoodoo and Ruby Rutabaker climbed into the back seat. With a sneer that could have stretched from Boston to Cape Cod, Cherry Tomato walked over to the hood ornament, snapping a handkerchief from her clutch bag. She stepped in front of Samson and Harry. Cherry dropped the sneer and breathed heavily onto the figurine. With a few strokes from the handkerchief, she polished the gold of any unsightly fingerprints.

Turning back to Harry and Samson, she put her handkerchief close to her face. While she glared at the two of them, Cherry blew her nose into the handkerchief and tossed it into the trash grid at the curb. Harry gagged when he saw what was in that handkerchief. "Bleech," he said.

117

"Let's go, Cherry!" yelled the mayor from the front window.

"Coming, Boss Man," Cherry cheerfully replied as she walked away from Samson and Harry. Once she got into the driver's seat, she gunned the engine. Instantly, the Phantom pulled away from the curb. The mayor and his entourage sped away.

With eyes of calm but steely resolve, Samson unbuttoned his purple cape. He held out the purple fabric in his right hand. SNAP!

"A B R A C A D A B R A," proclaimed Samson.

Samson cracked the cape like a bullwhip. "It is time for you to know the secret to the word," Samson said. "As you know, Harry, powerful magic is all about links. Abracadabra comes from the ancient Hebrew—*ab, ben,* and *ruach hakodesh.* You are linking the holy breath of the Great Magician with the wind and the power of the tides. If you are of pure heart, that utterance will allow the magic deep within

118

your heart to conjoin with the powers of the cosmos."

Stunned, Harry watched the purple cloth float upward into the atmosphere. "But the deep magic will only conjoin when the heart is simple and pure," Samson said. The cape went flat, like the throw rug in the Moon living room. As it hovered in the air, the fabric changed from velvet to metal, from purple to red.

"What is this?" Harry asked. His eyes were wide with wonder.

"It is what a pure heart and an ancient word has wrought. Harry, meet Impenetrable," said Samson.

"Hullo, Impenetrable," Harry softly said. He gulped. His empty throat contracted.

"It won't respond like Rabbit responds. But it will take orders," Samson said with an instructional tone.

"What's it for?"

"It's the way you'll follow those who borrow fire," Samson said. "You had better see what you are in for. That is if you have the stomach for this."

Harry looked at Samson. Samson read Harry's mind. "Just another arrow in my quiver," Samson said. "Get on it, boy. Impenetrable is fast, but not that fast. You need to follow that Phantom Lustro."

120

Harry grabbed the side of the hovering metal and hoisted himself onto the red platform. It felt cold.

"It's full glamour," Samson explained. "Today, we think of glamour as something fashionable. For thousands of years, glamour has been a charm that makes you invisible. Impenetrable will become whatever goodness needs. But it won't do any of your dirty work, Harry, so don't get any ideas or get sidetracked, which can happen to kids in the eighth grade. Rabbit will be there, of course. Now go, my boy, be impenetrable. Darkness will not touch you when you are cloaked in this."

At that very moment, a five-year-old girl stepped out of Sleepy Hollow Outfitters holding her mother's hand. The little girl's

121

mouth dropped to the sidewalk as she pointed.

"A wizard on a flying carpet!" the girl screamed.

Harry, from atop the red metal, locked eyes with the little girl on the sidewalk.

"Impenetrable, hide!" Harry said.

Instantly, Harry and the flying carpet disappeared from view.

"Impenetrable, follow that Phantom!"

At his command, there was a *whoosh* outside the Sleepy Hollow Magic Shoppe, then a pop like a crack of thunder. The hair of the little girl and her mom was blown back by the speed of Impenetrable's departure.

"Wow!" said the mom. "This is going to be one heckuva Halloween!

"It sure is," said Samson Dupree as he smiled at the mother and her little girl.

The mother looked at the man who stood on the sidewalk in his red slippers and plastic, golden crown.

"Madison, right?" asked Samson softly. The mother was thrown off guard.

"Er . . . yes . . . but how?"

"And this is your daughter, Phoebe?"

"That's me! I just saw a flying carpet like in *Aladdin!*" said the little girl.

"Isn't that wonderful?" said Samson. He turned to Madison and said sweetly, "Why don't you come in, Madison. I think Phoebe might be ready for a rabbit."

"Oh, yes, Mommy!" cried Phoebe.

"Who are you?" asked Madison Asherton.

"I am Samson Dupree, proprietor of the Sleepy Hollow Magic Shoppe."

"Can I have a bunny, Mommy, please?" said Phoebe as she tugged on her mother's skirt.

Madison Asherton pushed back the bangs that had gotten tangled in the wind of Impenetrable. She looked at Samson and then at the storefront with the sign above the picture window that clearly read The Sleepy Hollow Magic Shoppe.

"I don't recall this store ever being here," Madison said. "Or you, Samson, for that matter. Forgive me." Madison was frazzled as she looked back at Samson. "How long have you been here?"

"Forever," he answered.

"Forever? But . . ." Madison replied, now even more confused.

"Do not fear, Madison Asherton. You now have the eyes to see. You saw the

Impenetrable, did you not? Well, when you experience *that*, it is hard for you not to *see* me and my little magic shop. Won't you come in?" Samson said as he opened the windowed door to his shop for Madison and Phoebe.

"Does this mean I am getting a rabbit?" Phoebe said as she rushed through the door.

"I don't know, sweetie," replied Madison, absently. "You have to feed him and clean his cage."

"But Phoebe was already out of earshot, having dashed inside the Sleepy Hollow Magic Shoppe where infinite treasures and wonders filled the shelves.

"Not with my Rabbit," Samson replied.

"Then what do you feed your rabbit?" asked Madison.

"Love," Samson replied.

As she walked toward the door, Madison

125

saw the cheery striped awning suspended above the threshold, as bright as the sun on a summer's day. Madison Asherton proceeded inside Samson's world as the bell at the hinge of the door twinkled, and she discovered she was walking without touching the floor.

126

THE BORROWING FIRE

The Phantom Lustro pulled through the tall wrought iron gates of the Sleepy Hollow Cemetery. Unseen by anyone, Harry and Rabbit, riding on the Impenetrable, followed right behind the black luxury car. For a high-end automobile, the Phantom spewed out a lot of gray smoke.

"Blech," Harry said. "That dang car needs a tune up!"

Unlike the wind that blew across the sidewalks of Sleepy Hollow, the cemetery was still and quiet. Fingers of mist wrapped around some of the headstones as if pointing the way. Harry swallowed hard. But he was okay. He could handle creepy.

Harry and Rabbit sat on the thin steel pad of the Impenetrable, hovering in place above a small green knoll. They watched as the mayor and his friends stepped out of the car. But BooBoo HooDoo, Cherry Tomato, and Ruby Rutabaker were no longer wearing loud skirts and high heels.

They wore dark hooded robes and black boots with silver buckles.

"How did they change like that?" Harry whispered to Rabbit.

"Black magic," Rabbit replied as the whip-fast Impenetrable settled down for a hover in the graveyard. With his front two paws, Rabbit smoothed his Harlequin lop ears that had gotten messed up in the wind during the departure from the magic store.

"Who's that?" asked Harry. He watched as a hooded figure stepped out of the car wearing a red satin mask to cover his face. The satin gleamed in the sunny graveyard. Only his eyes could be seen.

"Guess who? Your mayor," said Rabbit.

129

"What's with the mask?"

"Part of the darkness thing," replied Rabbit.

Harry raised his eyebrows. He stared at Rabbit. "You are pretty knowledgeable, aren't you?"

"You have to be when fighting evil," said Rabbit with a sigh. "Unfortunately."

Harry and Rabbit watched from the Impenetrable. In his red mask and hooded cloak, the mayor led the hooded women to a distant open grave where two scruffy guys in overalls waited. Harry watched as the workers laughed while taking some folded bills from the masked mayor.

"They seem awfully chummy," said Harry.

"They've done this before. The We Drive By Night Company has a lucrative side business with those twins, the Bittenbenders. They are your standard grave looters. After funerals, the Bittenbenders remove all the jewelry and keepsakes from the corpses before they seal them in the ground."

"That's so wrong," said Harry sadly.

"Tell me about it," Rabbit said.

Satisfied with the transaction, the Bittenbenders walked away from the open grave.

"Why have they reopened a grave?" Harry asked. "Haven't they taken all the loot?"

"This is a different business involving the mayor and the Bittenbenders. You may not have the stomach for this next part."

"Hey, I'm a man," Harry said.

"I warned you," Rabbit said. As Harry and Rabbit watched, the mayor mumbled a few words over the open grave. After every few mumblings, the hooded women replied in a song that Harry could not quite make out.

Suddenly, Harry shrieked at what he saw. The hooded man in the red satin mask turned his face up toward the Impenetrable and toward Harry's voice.

"It's just the wind, Boss Man," said Cherry Tomato.

"It's never just the wind," replied the hooded mayor through his red mask, scanning the landscape with his beady eyes. But hard as he tried, the mayor could see nothing. After all, he was looking right at the Impenetrable, cloaked in transparency, which hovered over the green hill.

If the mayor could have seen, he would have observed a very large rabbit putting his paw over Harry's mouth to silence him.

"Oh my gosh, that's Mrs. Kenyon from fourth-grade geometry," Harry whispered.

"Yes," said Rabbit, "She was a terrific teacher. She was very helpful with your troubles with isosceles triangles, don't you think?"

"Yeah, she really straightened me out on those congruent legs and base angle theories!" said Harry as he looked on in horror.

"She died of natural causes five months ago," said Rabbit.

"Well, it looks like Mrs. Kenyon's back and kicking," said Harry. He watched as the old teacher stood up from the grave. "Look, she's alive!"

"No, that kind of stuff only happens in

video games," said Rabbit. "Your mayor and his fun party have summoned something evil. It is the darkness that has animated her. Mrs. Kenyon's body is not alive again. Only the Great Magician can do something like that!"

"Oh my gosh!" Harry screamed again through Rabbit's paw, which muffled his shouts. "They took off her hand! Look, the body fell back into the grave! What in the world are they doing!"

133

Rabbit shrugged.

"Once darkness has what it wants," said Rabbit, "it drops you like a hot potato." Rabbit spoke in a matter-of-fact tone. He sighed. "Or, as in Mrs. Kenyon's case," Rabbit said, "they drop you like a cold corpse."

"Look, they are running away with her hand," Harry whispered in horror.

"Think this is a blessing?" Rabbit asked.

"No!" Harry said from his seat on the Impenetrable. "It is a curse!"

"You haven't seen anything yet, my dear, dear friend," said Rabbit. Then the Harlequin rabbit thought for a moment. "You ever think about blessings, Harry? When someone says 'God bless you' or 'Bless you, my boy'?"

"What about it?" Harry said, frightened.

"It's an expression of wonder. Bless you. Bless me. A blessing immediately transforms the atmosphere. It is like fresh flowers coming into a room, it makes the air so lovely."

"And a curse?" asked Harry.

"It changes the atmosphere too," Rabbit said softy. "But not in the same way."

"I shouldn't think so," Harry said.

"Well, they are preparing the curse with a hand from the dead."

135

On the stealth power of Samson Dupree's magical cape, which had become a red flying machine, Harry Moon continued his quest to get to the truth about the bonfire. As he had told his friend, Hao, Harry was pretty much convinced it was some kind of dark enchantment, but he had to be sure before he took it down with his own "good mischief."

The Impenetrable traveled across town, following the Phantom Lustro. When the car arrived at the towering gates of the mayor's Folly Farm, Harry and Rabbit flew over the gates on the Impenetrable, above the wrought iron spikes, arriving on the other side of them.

Folly Farm was the vast commercial concern of Mayor Kligore and the Kligorian Dynasty. Not only was Folly Farm the commercial property of the We Drive By Night Company, it was also the residence of the mayor and his family. The mayor's sons were the infamous bullies of the Sleepy Hollow school system. There was Titus in Harry's grade, tall and terrible. The other one was older. He was the dreadful Marcus Caligula Kligore, who was a senior and despicable to the core. Harry Moon had been to the awful Folly Farm grounds many times, but still he was overwhelmed by its vastness and seductive evil.

Through the sunny, rumbling air, Harry and Rabbit followed the car to an old stone courtyard on the Folly Farm property. From a distance, Harry watched as the door opened on the Phantom.

It was not the mayor and the band of grave robbers who stepped from the car.

It was the hand.

It jumped from the Phantom Lustro and landed on the stone of the courtyard. Like a fleshy spider, with fingers as feet, the hand scurried across the courtyard.

"Who or what In the world is that thing?" Harry said.

"Well, it appears to be Mrs. Kenyon's hand," Rabbit said, watching. "But it is a darkness from the spiritual realm. The hand is just a tool, a vessel for bad mischief. It is not really alive. It is being animated by black magic."

Harry winced an "Ugh" in disgust as if a bad smell had just crawled up his nose. "That's worse than bad, Rabbit. That's unholy, to do what they did with Mrs. Kenyon."

"It's not her, Harry. Mrs. Kenyon's soul has long passed from this realm."

"So disrespectful of the dead."

131

"Darkness has been around for thousands of years. It uses body parts like a mechanic uses wrenches."

"It doesn't make it right," Harry said, angry. He shook his head.

"It sure doesn't," said Rabbit.

They watched as the hand picked up the stick of wood that was left for it on the stone floor. The hand pressed the stick against a flat gray stone where the tinder nest rested. Twisting the stick hard in the grasp of its fingers, the hand turned, suspended in the air, working to produce a spark.

As the hooded women and the mayor stepped from the car, Harry observed that one of the hooded figures was carrying a hammered silver bowl in her hands.

"That's the bowl I saw in my dream!" said Harry.

"Yes, darkness has been using it for years,"

138

said Rabbit.

"I'm going to make sure that fire doesn't get started!" Harry said as he pulled his wand from his jeans. Harry had a hard energy in his face as he pulled the wand up into the air and began to speak out, "A B R A C A . . ."

"I think you better wait on that," Rabbit said as he waved his paw in front of Harry.

139

"Why wait? Stop the bonfire now, before everything gets started," said Harry as he raised his wand once again. "A B R A C A . . ."

"You do what you want," Rabbit said, interrupting Harry's command. "You have free will, and as far as I'm concerned, you are a man."

"Gee, thanks, Rabbit."

"However, this bonfire enchantment has been mesmerizing the town folk for years. It's how the unsuspecting folks of Sleepy Hollow have been blinded to Mayor Kligore's greed."

"They don't have free will?"

"That's what a curse is, Harry. Darkness denies what light has given all, the understanding to see life clearly. The only way to break a curse like this, which the town has been under for some fifteen years, is to break it while it is actually happening."

"How do I do that?" Harry asked as he watched the tinder nest on the stone smoke with heat, igniting in a small flame.

"Crack it like an egg," Rabbit said.

"Kinda like Samson cracked his cape?"

"Show the bonfire who is boss," Rabbit growled. He turned to Harry and scowled at him. "Use the ancient word that Samson has shown you and align it with the decency of your courageous heart."

"Wow!" Harry said, suddenly taken aback. "I

have never seen you like this! You don't mess around."

"I'm the light of the Great Magician, Harry," Rabbit said.

"I know," replied Harry.

"I don't mess around," Rabbit said. "Except when it comes to Oink. He annoys me."

"He annoys me too," Harry said.

141

"Normally, I would turn the other cheek."

"Right," said Harry.

"But Oink's a demon. He renounced me long ago and you know what that means."

"What, exactly?"

"There's no turning back for him."

Harry pulled back from Rabbit because the riled-up furry thing of his conscience was right at his nose.

Harry was anxious to change the subject, for he did not like to see such hard anger in Rabbit. He looked over Rabbit's shoulder from the Impenetrable to see the silver bowl now filled with fire. The hand was on the ground.

"What will they do with that hand, I wonder?" said Harry.

142

"The mayor forgot to get Cherry Tomato a birthday gift. Remember? That's how this all started."

Rabbit turned away from Harry, and Harry was grateful for a tad less tension in the air. Harry and Rabbit looked out at the courtyard from the platform of steel.

"He's going to surprise her with a gift now. Watch," Rabbit said.

"Whatdyamean? He's gonna give her the dead hand?" Harry asked, looking at the hooded entourage still gathered in the courtyard.

"Behold," Rabbit said.

The hooded Mayor Kligore pulled off the red satin mask from his face. He laughed.

"How do you know what's going to happen?" Harry asked.

"I know evil," said Rabbit

"And demons, apparently," Harry said, raising his eyebrows.

As Mayor Kligore laughed, he sang an odd verse over the courtyard. Harry watched as a short, stubby man in a hospital-green apron came through a door and onto the courtyard. He walked toward the mayor.

"Who's that?" asked Harry.

"The jeweler," answered Rabbit.

Harry squinted to see better as the jeweler

in the green apron picked up the severed hand. He mumbled something over its fingers and then blew on it. The remaining flesh from the hand fell away.

"Ugh," said Harry. "This is awful."

"What did Samson tell you? Whether a blessing or curse, it changes the atmosphere."

"Even me?" Harry said.

144

"You're part of the atmosphere, Harry, aren't you? You breathe in and out, don't you? By the way, you're changing it too, as I speak."

Harry turned his eyes back to the courtyard. He squinted again as the jeweler continued his odd mumblings. With his ugly mouth, the jeweler blew on the skeleton hand that he held in his paw. The bones broke apart and gathered in the air.

"Hey," said Harry, shocked to his bones. "That's no jeweler! That's Oink!"

"A demon of many talents," said Rabbit.

The bone chips swirled in the air above the courtyard. As the swirling increased in velocity, the chips became small spheres and gathered into a strand. Cherry's face beamed in delight as a gleaming pearl necklace appeared around her neck.

"Pearls before swine," said Rabbit.

"Blech." Harry winced. "Gross."

"Such darkness is a gross endeavor," Rabbit said in an affirming tone.

From the red pad of the Impenetrable, Harry and Rabbit could hear the distant voices of the group.

"They are beautiful, Boss Man," Cherry said, handling the pearls with her fingers. "Thank you!"

"I apologize for my birthday present being late," said Mayor Maximus Kligore.

"Even demons, in their unholy mischief,

can be polite," said Rabbit.

✧

"Ta da!" Honey Moon proclaimed as she twirled for Harry. Once again, she entered his bedroom without knocking. She was in her Cleopatra wig and costume. It was just after dinner and only a few hours before the bonfire lighting.

"What do you think?" she said.

"I'll get my jacket," said Harry.

"No need," Honey said. "I have worked it out with Mom. I told her that you in your no-costume attire would totally wreck the illusion of Cleopatra and her mighty chariot. Besides, Liam and Mason are in the sixth grade, and their friend Oliver is joining us. Oliver is in high school. He is playing Bucephalus, my mighty stallion. I shall be well looked after."

Honey deigned to kiss her brother on the cheek. "Adieu, bro-there, my chariot doth await!" And with that, Honey theatrically exited the room with a flourish.

Harry looked out the window at the street below. There were lots of trick-or-treaters running through the streets. He saw Mason and Liam in breastplates and helms next to Honey's once-red wagon. It had been spray painted gold. In Harry's mind, it looked pretty lame. There was some poor guy in a horse outfit pulling the wagon chariot as Honey jumped in.

147

"Geesh," Harry said.

"Don't worry," Rabbit said as he came to the window and put his arm around Harry. "I got you covered."

"What do you mean?" said Harry.

"You and me, we're going to beat this thing together," answered Rabbit. "Besides, you now know the secret of Abracadabra. You can bring the power of the tides and the force of the wind to the tip of your wand."

⌒∿⌒

John Moon and Mary Moon were at the front door of the Moon home, greeting the trick-or-treaters who flooded the hallway. John wore a vampire outfit with fake, bloody fangs. Mary was in a pink gown and tiara with fiberglass slippers. She was Cinderella.

From the doorway, John watched as Harry made his way through the crowd of trick-or-treaters in the hallway. John called out to Harry, but Harry did not hear. He seemed oblivious to everything and everyone.

148

Mary took John's hand as they watched Harry walk alone down the street jammed with little kids in costumes. "What's with Harry, any-ways?" John said to Mary.

"Growing pains," Mary said with a small smile.

"Sometimes, Mary, I don't know. Is Harry foolish or a genius?" John asked, mumbling through a mouth full of fake, bloody fangs.

"Genius," Mary said as she watched Harry walk down Nightingale Lane. "We just have to love him, John. We just have to help him turn his own pages."

"It's those pages, Mary, that worry me."

"Those pages are his destiny, John. He has an appointment that he needs to keep," Mary said.

The Clock Tower in the town square struck eight. The street lamps that surrounded Main Street blinked on and off. The Halloween curfew was in effect. The fire trucks from Sleepy Hollow, Cambridge, and Boston surrounded the square.

149

The town square was filled with the citizens of Sleepy Hollow. The vendors—apple cider, donut dunking, stews and soups—were all doing great business.

The traditional Bone Band, musicians from the local theatre group, played in the gazebo. They wore skeleton costumes. With the striking of eight from the clock tower, the square flooded with even more folks and all the trick-or-treaters.

In all the chaos, Harry Moon's eyes were focused on the silver bowl that rested between the two high school students, who wore advent crowns and white robes, standing at the steps of the gazebo. As the crowd gathered, Mayor Maximus Kligore took the stand and talked about the tradition of the winter light that ushered in the end of the harvest.

"Listen to him go on," Harry said to Rabbit. "Well, this is the last stop for your winter light, buddy." As the band played, the two high schoolers stood. Harry pulled out the wand to snuff the light.

"Now remember," Rabbit whispered to Harry. "You can't break the curse until the curse is in process. Then snap it like a whip with your wand. Do not get distracted by the powers that war against you!"

No sooner had Rabbit said those words

than Honey, in her full golden-Cleopatra regalia, came running at Harry, wailing. Her blue Egyptian-like mascara was streaking from the tears, and her wig was falling down her tiny back.

"Help! Help, Harry Moon! Bucephalus has gone crazy! He's trampling the gladiators! Please, Harry, you have to stop him!"

For the first time, Rabbit's line, "Don't worry, I got you covered," made sense to Harry. He was going to need some help, and fast. As Harry ran past the green-pea soup booth, there in front of him were the two sixth graders, Mason and Liam, on the ground. The gold-painted wagon had been overturned and flattened into a sheet. Liam's breastplate had been torn from his chest, and Mason had thrown his hands in front of his face as the costumed horse rose up high over the boys and stomped its front legs toward them.

"A B R A C A D A B R A!" shouted Harry, raising his wand against the hooded stallion.

151

"YOU DARE SAY ABRACADABRA TO ME!" shouted the stallion at Harry. The horse was no ordinary costumed horse. Its hideous eyes went yellow when it saw Harry. As the stallion's front legs came slamming down with a ferocious fury onto Mason, they were swiped aside by a green rod that shot out from Harry's almond-wood wand.

"Run, Mason!" shouted Harry.

152

Mason rolled underneath the rod and away from the stallion. But the dragon horse had other plans. It had set its yellow eyes on Harry.

Its head sparking with yellow embers, the steed charged at Harry. As Harry moved to get clear of his attacker, he stumbled. His wand fell, rolling beneath the Haunted Wood Brasserie booth.

Harry skittered to the ground. Without his wand, he braced himself for the weighty trampling of this terrible *thing*. Honey Moon screamed. The costumed stallion was upon Harry.

And as fast as you could say Sleepy Hollow Magic Shoppe a phantom creature bound out from behind Harry. "I've got your back!" roared a voice, a thunderous sound Harry had never heard before. The creature was massive. Rabbit's eyes flashed with power that seemed unstoppable.

"I MESS WITH YOU! YOU DON'T MESS WITH ME!" roared Rabbit.

The black-and-white lagomorph rose as tall as the Clock Tower. His jaw clamped down on the stallion and threw him clear of Harry. The horse costume melted as it hit the trunk of an elm. Beneath the costume was Oink. Whimpering, but not wanting to be exposed, the ugly dog slinked behind the tree and slunk back into darkness.

153

"Harry! Harry Moon!"

Harry turned at the calling of his name. "I told you not to get distracted!" Harry saw Rabbit picking up his wand by the Brasserie booth. His friend had returned to his normal size, about waist high to Harry, no longer the ginormous rescuer.

WHOOSH! Harry turned again. This time he swiveled at the sound of his powerful wand.

Rabbit had thrown the instrument through the air, and it was already sailing. Harry reached up and snatched it deftly as he spun.

"Break it, Harry. Crack it open like an egg!" Rabbit shouted. "Release its poison!" As Harry looked to the center of the square, he saw the hammered silver bowl being turned upside down by the senior boys. The fire fell on the tinder nest. Only this particular tinder nest was two stories high buried inside the massive town square scaffolding!

WOVROOOM!

The bonfire erupted. The flames scampered up the pine scaffolding. The leaves billowed white smoke in the heat. The blaze consumed the tower. Just as in Harry's dream, the people of Sleepy Hollow gathered around the enormous conflagration. The applause rose as the flames crawled to the peak of the wood construction. The Bone Band at the gazebo played, adding weight to a ritual they did not even realize they were part of.

The swirling smoke from the leaves made it almost impossible for Harry to see. If the people were becoming the dragons he witnessed in his nightmares, he wouldn't know. In the distance, he heard the tiny tinkling of the bell from the Sleepy Hollow Magic Shoppe. It seemed to be his only true north in the wall of gray-and-white smoke, as if the town green were a smoldering battlefield.

155

Harry ran away from the square. As he stepped clear of the eye of the smoky curse, Harry saw the Sleepy Hollow Magic Shoppe. The front door was ajar, causing the bell to ring. Directly in front of him, just as it had been only hours ago when Harry had visited Samson, Harry spied the mayor's luxury car.

Without a thought, Harry jumped onto the hood of the car, pulling himself up past the windshield and onto the roof of the Phantom Lustro. From there, Harry could see the crowning trees of elm and maple that surrounded the square. He saw the ring of red fire trucks surrounding the square.

156

Atop the hood of the car, Harry spread his legs to anchor himself. He took a deep breath to find the deep magic at the center of his heart. He thought about all that Samson had taught him and how the powerful magic was linked to the tremendousness of the wind and the pull of the ocean tides. He searched for the goodness inside of him, at the root of his life-giving heart. He focused his attention on the tip of his wand. He concentrated his efforts to link and connect the energies of his own being with the holy breath and the power of nature at the very tip of the wand.

"A B R A C A D A B R A!" Harry shouted as he raised his wand into the sky.

He spread his arms like wings. He plunged his wand deeper into the air. He felt the reverence of that single word, Abracadabra. As he did, the tip of the wand seemed to command the trees. For as he lowered the wand with his right hand, the crowns of the maple and elm trees seemed to bow to the ground, obeying the deep, mysterious magic of his wand. As the trees bent low, the tops of the trees burst into flames from the bonfire.

Unseen by Harry, Samson Dupree had stepped out of the magic store and watched the Sleepy Hollow miracle unfold.

"What the heck!" Fire Chief Mike Orize shouted as he watched the maple and elm trees catch fire in the middle of the square.

158

On the radio, the chief barked out orders to the other engines. Almost instantly, the sky above the square was filled with the spray of seventeen different hoses.

The water fell across the crowd, and they blinked awake, confused. They looked around, trying to make sense of the commotion happening all around. In her wet Cinderella gown, Mary Moon blinked, squinting about as the bonfire diminished. She looked for her family. She looked for Harry.

There in the distance, atop the Phantom Lustro, Mary Moon saw her son.

He stood there, high above the sidewalk, his legs apart, like a hero from a movie. She could only see his silhouette, water dripping from his sleeves. But she knew him anywhere, for there in the silhouette was his unruly hair and in his right hand was the wand. At that very moment, she understood, finally, who her son would be. Not an executive at Google. Not a doctor at Mass General. But a warrior of light against the darkness.

For all her pondering, Mary Moon discovered the treasure of a deep wisdom. You might be gifted with music or dance or science or hospitality or be a great follower or a great leader. It was imprinted in your hand. You had no control over your gift.

But your destiny, that is what you do control. For destiny is how you use the gifts that you were given. And Harry Moon was in the midst of his destiny. For the first time, Mary Moon could look on the silhouette of her boy and know who he was.

He was magic. For what, and why, she might never know the fullness of it. But, as the voice had told her at Old North Church, Harry would be just fine.

Water unfurled from the hoses onto the square. The flames in the trees were expunged. The bonfire was extinguished. The people watching were no longer tethered to the mesmerizing flames.

∾

"Get off my car!" the fierce Mayor Kligore yelled up at Harry.

"I was just wiping the water from it, sir," Harry said as he slid down the Phantom, leaving a car that was completely dry.

"Get out of my way, punk!" shouted Cherry Tomato.

"Hey, what's that?" Harry asked as he

looked up at her necklace. Cherry tried to cover the pearls, wondering what the magic boy had seen.

"What?" she asked.

"Oh," he exclaimed, "it's something that doesn't belong to you!" With that, he reached up and yanked the strand of pearls that the mayor had belatedly given her for her birthday.

"Boss Man!" Cherry shouted as she pointed at Harry. "He took my pearls. My beautiful pearls!"

161

"Get in the car, Cherry. I'll get you new ones," the mayor yelled as he climbed into the passenger side.

"But I liked those, Boss!" she whined, grabbing at her neck as if she was suddenly naked.

"Drive!" he ordered.

With that, Cherry had no choice but to

open the car door and take the wheel. The car swerved, leaping from the curb. It was trying to run Harry down. He fell across the grill and bounced upward, grabbing the golden hood ornament as his anchor. Holding on for dear life, Harry found himself staring directly at the mayor through the windshield.

"Happy Halloween!" Harry shouted, locking eyes with the mayor on the other side of the glass.

162

There was no response, except the car jerked suddenly and Harry was thrown from the sinister vehicle like a rag doll.

CRAACK! went the sound as Harry flew from the anchor of the Flying Lady ornament. He tumbled onto the sidewalk. Harry rolled to a stop among the fragments of the broken wings of the Spirit of Desire.

In her glittering Cleopatra outfit with her two gladiators, bloodied but unbowed, trailing beside her, Honey ran to Harry.

"Are you all right, Harry? I'll never be Cleopatra again, I promise! I wanna grow up. No more costumes for me, either! I want to be just like you!" she cried as she threw her arms around Harry. "Please, I'll wear normal clothes! I am a magnet for danger when I dress like the queen of Egypt!"

"Don't grow up too fast, Honey," Harry said to her softly and even with some warmth. He did not really like his sister, but he loved her. "Promise me?"

"Okay!" she said as she cried. The two gladiators hugged Harry as well. "We promise Harry, we won't grow up too fast, either!" they bawled. Harry just shook his head. Kids.

Across the street, Harry Moon saw Dracula and Cinderella waiting for him on the town green. He smiled at his parents. He put his wand in his back pocket. He just wanted to be a kid for a minute. As Honey ran from the sidewalk, Harry followed her over to the green where his family was.

John Moon held Harvest Moon under his right arm and held Mary's hand with his left. Honey rushed to her mom and took her left hand.

"Wanna walk home with us?" John Moon asked Harry as he reached them.

"You know," said Mary Moon to Harry, "we Nightingale Knights aren't really knights without their knight in shining armor."

Harry hesitated for a moment. "I really want to, Mom."

Mary looked at him. "I know you do."

"But there's just a little something I have to take care of tonight. I promise you both," Harry said as he looked to his dad, "it's not dangerous."

165

"See you at home, then?" John said.

"See you at home," Harry said.

With that, Harry turned and ran down Main Street. Despite the fire engines and police cars and people headed home, all that Mary could see was her son, running down the road. And there ahead of him was the great golden moon in the now silent night.

Mary then looked over at John, who was

shaken. A tear rolled down his cheek as he watched his son disappear into the moonlit night.

"What's wrong, sweetheart?" she asked.

"Growing pains," he replied.

Harry crept slowly through the Sleepy Hollow Cemetery. A choir of owls was hoohooing, greeting the returning magician.

Harry passed Author's Ridge where Nathaniel Hawthorne, Louisa May Alcott, Henry David Thoreau, and Ralph Waldo Emerson were all buried within a few yards of one another. He thought of the hymn from Old North Church, the song about hearing God in the grass. He was sure that Thoreau and Emerson would have really liked that song.

He arrived at the gravestone he was searching for. The grass near the stone had recently been disturbed. He knelt down and read the modest stone to make sure that he was where he was supposed to be.

Finally, he said, "I don't know how to talk to you because I know you are not really here. I hope you are in a place of wonder, Mrs. Kenyon. Rabbit was right. You didn't chew me out when I couldn't figure out those congruent legs in math class. I will always be grateful."

He pulled out his wand and softly incanted, "A B R A C A D A B R A." He turned the wand in his hand as the tip of it conjoined with the many powers of heart, breath, and nature. Slowly the earth opened beneath the disturbed grass.

He pulled the pearls from Cherry Tomato's necklace from his pocket. "I am not sure that it matters wherever you are, Mrs. Kenyon, but I wanted you to have your hand back, in case you needed it."

He dropped the pearls into the small hole and filled it with soil and grass.

"You know, I want to do right by you cause you always did right by me. Bless you, Mrs. Kenyon. I look forward to seeing you again one day."

168

WINGS

The funny thing about life is that nothing ever stays the same. Nothing ever really goes back to the way it was before. The universe expands. Babies grow. Houses get remodeled. Eighth graders graduate to high school. "The only permanent thing in life is change," Benjamin Franklin once said. Tales and stories change.

In the case of Sleepy Hollow, the stories don't change, they simply fade with age.

When Monday's edition of *Awake in Sleepy Hollow* arrived at front doors across the little New England town, the headline story about the out-of-control bonfire that forced the fire department to get to work was already fading from the front page of the paper.

"Dang cheap ink!" said Fire Chief Mike Orize as he stood in his robe Monday morning at his kitchen counter reading about the bonfire. Chief Mike could barely make out the words about the battalions of men and women who had worked together with Cambridge and Boston to hose down the fire.

He squinted to read in little tiny print the reports of what he had also seen, that the branches of the maple and elm trees had magically changed and that the treetops had mysteriously bent closer to the fire, which forced the bonfire to spread dramatically, causing the fire trucks to leap into action and douse the bonfire with water, breaking this particular curse.

But, it was another story that shaped the news that morning. "It had been a dry autumn," Mayor Maximus Kligore was quoted as saying in the paper, "and the leaves and branches in the square were particularly vulnerable to high temperature."

Chief Mike shook his head, for nowhere in the article did it mention Harry Moon and the command of Abracadabra that had seemed to transform the trees, bringing them lower to the ground.

Even though the bonfire story was the headline, it seemed to Chief Mike Orize that the near catastrophic bonfire on Halloween night would not be remembered as such a big story after all. Because of the mayor's comments, Chief Mike figured the heroics of his station would probably be forgotten by Christmas.

After all, there was no real damage from the fire. Thankfully, there were no fatalities. No one was hurt. *No*, thought Chief Mike Orize as he watched the story fade before his eyes, *the truth in Sleepy Hollow was never ever really much of a story at all.*

But Sleepy Hollow would not have to fight its battles alone. It had been given a hero. Over the ages, whether King Arthur, Robin Hood, or Iron Man, heroes have always been a selfless lot. They reach beyond their own concerns and put the people first.

Harry Moon was always putting others first. And while his mom and dad fretted, he knew that he had to drive an arrow through the dark magic of the annual Sleepy Hollow Halloween bonfire.

"Curses take time to untangle," Samson Dupree, in his purple robe and crown, said to Harry the next day as they watched the last of the bonfire banners and the tents get loaded into trucks on the village square. "You have made a start here by ending the bonfire before the people in this town could be mesmerized.

"Things will begin to change in Sleepy Hollow, Harry Moon. Evil will not have its way." Samson patted the young magician on his back.

"Things always change, Harry. The only thing that doesn't change is the goodness found in heroes. A hero is a hero forever."

"Do you think stopping the fire early really mattered?" asked Harry.

"It does, Harry. Maybe this Christmas there will be a few less witch and ghoul ornaments in the display windows, maybe a few less dragon-red eggs rolling down the hills at next year's Easter egg hunt at Melville Field. The treasured vortex in this town, which you will one day know more about, has been preserved. It's a beginning," Samson said. "And beginnings can lead to great things, Harry Moon."

173

∽∾∽

That Sunday, the shiny black Phantom Lustro owned by Maximus Kligore, once again prowled the sunny streets on worship day. In all his regal countenance, Mayor Kligore sat proudly in the black leather passenger seat while Cherry Tomato drove.

"Do you know the word that I have been thinking about, Cherry?" Maximus asked as they drove past the Old North Church at the corner of Mt. Sinai Road and Nathaniel Hawthorne Road.

"What's that, Boss Man?" asked Cherry Tomato.

"Impenetrable," he said, sighing deeply, letting it roll off his tongue as if he was describing the rarest and most delicious chocolate known to humankind.

"Im-pen-er-tree-ble," Cherry said.

"That's right," the mayor said, slouching back in his seat. "That's who we are. Impenetrable. Nothing. Nothing will stop us."

"Impenetrable," Cherry said more quickly, liking the sound of it. "That's right, Boss Man, we drive by night and we are impenetrable."

"Exactly," he replied.

The hood of the car passed the Old North Church where the parishioners sang a mighty chorus. The car was shiny and bright as usual. The hood ornament of the Lustro for over a hundred years, however, had changed. Harry Moon had clipped off its golden wings

The golden lady hood ornament looked poised to launch into the sky, unaware that she did not possess the wings to get her where she needed to go.

Harry had gathered those gold wings from the sidewalk and sent them to Perpetual Help Church outside Boston. The pastor there said the gold in the wings would pay for all the winter meals for their poor community. He did not know whom to thank for the gift, for when he received the package, there was no return address or sender.

Sometimes we see only what we want to see. Stories fade. The truth seems blurred. But still, the work of heroes is evident to those who have the eyes to see it.

Of course, Maximus and Cherry were not looking for the truth that lived with the parishioners inside the Old North Church.

176

Maximus and Cherry were making a drop off. The Lustro pulled over to the curb. Cherry jumped out of the car and opened the back passenger door so that Oink could depart.

"Make me proud," Maximus said.

"You got it, Daddy," replied Oink.

In her black Jimmy Choo heels, Cherry teetered back to the Phantom Lustro. She knew that Boss Man was hungry, and they were late. She and Maximus were headed to Omelet Circus in the neighboring town of Oxford. The Omelet Circus was offering an early two-for-one special. The mayor was rich, but he was also cheap.

As the Phantom Lustro pulled away, it left behind a stranger on the sidewalk, and it was not Samson Dupree.

For those who did not have the gift of sight, this was a little old lady in a pillbox hat carrying a tattered purse. This was someone in need. For those who had the eyes to see, this was Oink, the hound of hell, waiting to bring aboard some new recruits for the We Drive By Night Company.

Inside Old North, Harry and his family sat in the second pew, singing.

This is my Father's world.
O let me ne'er forget
That though the wrong
seems oft so strong,
God is the ruler yet.

178

Harry Moon's face looked harder, stronger as he belted out the words. Still, there were no whiskers on his chin. Mary Moon appeared to be a little wiser. Her hazel eyes had an extra glint in them. Honey Moon's chestnut hair was a little longer. Even Harvest Moon, as he hummed the tune in his dad's arms, seemed to look more like a child and less like a toddler.

And John Moon was sprouting a moustache. Like all of us, the Moon Family was changing.

But the one thing that was not changing

was the truth of what they were singing. To be loved by the Divine was a wonderful thing, and to be given a friend to guide us, encourage us, and chide us was better still.

And we should not be surprised if we are fortunate enough to meet up with that friend. Be it a stranger, a rabbit, a turtle, a whisper, a nudge, or even, sometimes, the magic of our own imagination.

Never, never ever be surprised.

179

A B R A C A D A B R A.

180

MARK ANDREW POE

Harry Moon author Mark Andrew Poe never thought about being a children's writer growing up. His dream was to love and care for animals, specifically his friends in the rabbit community.

Along the way, Mark became successful in all sorts of interesting careers. He entered the print and publishing world as a young man, and his company did really, really well.

181

Mark became a popular and nationally sought-after health care advocate for the care and well-being of rabbits.

Years ago, Mark came up with the idea of a story about a young man with a special connection to a world of magic, all revealed through a remarkable rabbit friend. Mark worked on his idea for several years before building a collaborative creative team to help bring his idea to life. And Harry Moon was born.

In 2014, Mark began a multi-book print series project intended to launch *The Adventures of Harry Moon* into the youth marketplace as a hero defined by a love for a magic where love and 'DO NO EVIL' live. Today, Mark continues to work on the many stories of Harry Moon. He lives in suburban Chicago with his wife and his twenty-five rabbits.

BE SURE TO READ THE CONTINUING AND AMAZING ADVENTURES OF HARRY MOON

Harry Moon's
DNA

Helps his fellow schoolmates
Makes friends with those who had once been his enemies
Respects nature
Honors his body
Does not categorize people too quickly
Seeks wisdom from adults
Guides the young
Controls his passions
Is curious
Understands that life will have trouble and accepts it
And, of course, loves his mom!

SEE HOW IT ALL STARTED WITH THE ORIGIN STORY!

POSTER INSIDE!

HARRY MOON

ORIGIN

WAND-PAPER-SCISSORS

DO NO EVIL

MARK ANDREW POE

POSTER INSIDE!

HARRY MOON

HARRY'S CHRISTMAS CAROL

POSTER INSIDE!

HARRY MOON

TICKLISH

MARK ANDREW POE

Coming
Soon!

HARRY MOON
PROFESSOR EINSTONE
POSTER INSIDE!

HARRY MOON
FIRST LIGHT
POSTER INSIDE!

FOR MORE BOOKS
& RESOURCES GO TO
HARRYMOON.COM

Honey Moon's
DNA

Builds friendships that matter
Goes where she is needed
Helps fellow classmates
Speaks Her mind
Honors her body
Does not categorize others
Loves to have a blast
Seeks wisdom from adults
Desires to be brave
Sparkles away
And, of course, loves her mom

HONEY MOON
SCARY LITTLE CHRISTMAS

POSTER INSIDE!

HONEY MOON
DOG DAZE

POSTER INSIDE!

SOFI BENITEZ